BRICK OF SOUND 3

BY

MADISON PATE

BY

MADISON PATE

Printed in the United States of America by
T&J Publishers (Atlanta, GA.)
www.TandJPublishers.com

Cover design by Supply Graphics
Book format and layout by Timothy Flemming, Jr. (T&J Publishers)

ISBN: 979-8-218-11012-3

To contact author, go to:

Website: www.madison-pate.com
Email: contact@madison-pate.com
Facebook: Madison Pate
Instagram: Brick of Sound
LinkedIn: Madison Pate

This book is dedicated to my uncle and mentor
Katahj Copley. Thank you for all of the life
advice and just about everything else.

TABLE OF CONTENTS

BACK TO SCHOOL (SOMEWHAT)

Is this a living nightmare? Is this constant dream going to ever end? Madison had this dream every night, not knowing what it meant.

"Blood. It's on my hands." She thought, looking down. But before she could continue thinking, her hands became blurry in her vision. Her eyes were filled with tears now.

"It's the only dream I don't have control over. I can't stop it." Madison looked up to the sky, which was blood red. She let out a scream, which seemed to shake the earth, or wherever she was, itself. Madison then shot up, now awake, in a cold sweat.

"Same dream?" Hope questioned her. She was in a better state than when Madison saw her for the first time.

"Yeah. We've got to escape sooner or later."

Now on Earthland

"So, there's no way that we can get her back, right?" Allie asked everyone in the room, with her arms crossed.

"If we tried, we would get banned. Even if we did return her, our dimension would be destroyed by the higher ups in the Land Beyond." Chloe answered.

"But we still don't know which one of us actually messed up the timeline! There's still hope!"

"It's a 50/50 chance. Ironically, Madison is the one who gives us our luck. Without her, we can't take many chances." Walter interrupted.

"Well, since you're all smart, why don't you use your Time Control to bring us to the future?" Mandy brought up, and everyone thought about it until Chloe got the idea.

"She's right! Time Control could open up an Air Portal to bring us through!"

"Using an Air Portal gives us the same chances as a Ground Portal. We don't know for sure if the future isn't destroyed like Epitomus." Allie said.

"Are you guys stupid? As long as Madison's there, it won't be destroyed." Kendall responded.

"Not exactly. The terrain of the future is destroyed to our knowledge, but we don't know if it's still occupied. There isn't much for her to protect." Mandy told him. Walter sighed, then walked off to the door.

"I'll just open up an Air Portal. Wait inside."

In the future

"Hands behind your back!" A voice from multiple soldiers said to Madison, all of them having guns pointed towards her. She did as told.

"Yeah yeah, I know." One of the many soldiers put Power Chains around her hands, and they then began escorting her to some base.

"I really want to meet the new tenor." She thought to herself, looking at the sky.

"I hope they're cool!"

Back on Earthland

"We're gonna get in so much trouble for this, especially you! You're not even supposed to be here!" Chloe exclaimed, pointing at Mandy. She simply crossed her arms.

"I'm just tagging along! After this, I'm leaving." Walter clapped his hands together, which opened up the portal. To make it larger, he slammed his hands on the ground, creating a similar earthquake to when Madison used her shockwaves correctly.

"If that were the case, Brandon would be here too. But here we are!" Kendall countered.

"Come on guys, stop arguing! We'll resolve this later. First, we got to bring her back!" Allie interrupted, jumping high enough to get into the portal, soon followed by Walter.

"Don't just leave us behind!" Kendall used his Half Phoenix form to fly through the portal, then followed by Chloe and Mandy. The portal closed up, which made a loud noise, as it was then followed by a large firework. Ms. Martinez rushed outside.

"What the heck was that noise?" Elizabeth was also outside, since she caused the large firework.

"I was just practicing."

"Makes sense." Ms. Martinez returned back to her office in the now fully built Band House Extended.

Now in the future

Everyone who was on the mission appeared out of a portal from the ground, which launched them upwards. They all screamed until they eventually landed around each other.

"Oh. So it is still active."

Chapter 1

NEW IMPROVEMENTS

"Haha, this cell is hot." Madison said, probably while talking to herself. She was staring at the wall, plotting some sort of plan in her head.

"I should just break out now, but I can't use any of my powers. Guess I have to go back to ground zero." She thought, beginning to stand up.

In a ruined city

"The Tenor Detector says that we should go this way." Kendall told the group behind them, while pointing to the left.

"What the heck is a Tenor Detector?" Allie questioned him, and he pointed towards a watch like device on his arm.

"I put a tracker on the harness she wore all the time!"

"Why would you do that?"

"Just in case she got lost in a building again."

"Again?"

"Focus, guys. We've gotta get her home to us before we run out of time." Chloe interrupted, still following them. The Tenor Detector began going haywire, as they had hit the jackpot apparently.

"It's in the ground below? Stand back, I got this." Allie began, cracking her knuckles.

Below them

"Idiot!" Madison exclaimed, kicking a soldier in the face. She began running through the corridors, dodging the oncoming bullets.

"You won't make it to the general's office!" One of them shouted out to her, as she turned around.

"Alright, take me down then!" She ran back towards them, using a knee like attack to knock one upwards. Two soldiers with swords charged at her, and swung the weapons in her direction. Madison flipped herself upside down, so she could kick the two using full force.

"Looks like the fly came out of their trap." The still unknown figure said, walking from the opposite end of the hallway.

"Yeah, I don't like getting caught. I'll show you what it means to be Powerful!" She smirked, getting ready to fight them. Before either of them could make a move, the metal from above them began denting rapidly. It completely crashed down, not revealing the figures clearly because of the smoke.

"I told you this is where she was!" Kendall said from inside the smoke. When it cleared, it showed the entire crew that was on the mission on top of the now broken slab of metal.

"You're not the tenor. This is totally not what I was imagining." Madison told them, still with her hands tied behind her back.

"Who cares? We still saved you. Hurry, before the stranger gets mad!" Walter interjected, reaching out a hand towards her. Madison, who of course couldn't grab it, made him grab the harness instead and pull them upwards.

"There's still one more person left."

As they arrived in Earthland

"We've gotta sneak into the newer Band House!" Chloe whispered, motioning to Walter for him to throw Madison through the door, but he didn't because of how stupid the idea was.

"What if we just like, teleported in there?" Madison asked, still being held onto from the harness.

"None of us can teleport a large amount of people, idiot!" Allie answered, as they dropped onto the ground.

"Let's just run in there! Three, Two, O-" Mandy began, before interrupted by the one they didn't want to see the most.

"Just what do you guys think you're doing?" Ms. Martinez interjected, sending a cold shock through all of them.

"We're just showing the Epitomus Madison around!" Walter lied, holding up Madison to her. She did some sort of salute.

"Full Speed Ahead!" Ms. Martinez crossed her arms, not believing any of it.

"Epitomus Madison has a scar on her face."

"Uh..."

"Let's book it!" Madison yelled, swinging herself towards the entrance to Band House Extended, which ended up dragging Walter with her. Everyone else followed close behind, until Ms. Martinez appeared in front of their possible escape.

"None of you guys are leaving until you explain yourselves."

"Alright, so basically we went to the future to find Madison, and we found her about to face off against that mystery person." Kendall explained, and everyone agreed.

"Didn't I tell all of you guys beforehand," Ms. Martinez began, as the others just stood in defeat.

"That if you went to save her, you would get banned?"

...

"So you're telling me there isn't a new tenor?! Ugh, what a rip off!" Madison complained, as Allie led her through the new building. "I would've expected you guys to have at least someone new while I was kidnapped again. It isn't exactly the most fun thing in the world, yknow."

"Tell me about it. Anyway, here's your room, right next to mine." She pointed at both of them in succession.

"...Man, and I thought this day couldn't get any worse."

"Quit mumbling and go to sleep!"

Chapter 2

TENOR AND BARI

"Hey kid, wanna buy some lettuce?" Madison said in her sleep, almost about to fall off her bed. The Band House Extended was wider than the normal one, but it held less people. Whoever the best of the best was able to live in it, and of course Madison was chosen.

"Wake up, idiot!" Allie shouted, throwing a rock at her. She managed to hit it away, but in turn, also woke up.

"Stop throwing random things at me!"

"We gotta go, bro! Make sure you get ready on time!" Chloe shouted from the door, then running out.

"Let's see. What plans do I have to make this year?" Madison thought to herself, starting to stand up.

"There's so many possibilities to plan out."

The Woodwind Class

"So, if last year was teaching us how to fight using our powers," Chloe began, looking around for the Bari.

"Then what are we gonna do this year?" Madison finished, glancing over to the Tenor shelves. There was the one Mandy used in the top shelf, and then the 2 other ones. Right next to this shelf, was the Bari case. They both ran to the section of the room.

"Guess what, bro?" Chloe questioned Madison, who gave her a thumbs up in response.

"We're the Tenor and Bari now, right?" She answered, and Chloe gave her a thumbs up.

"Yeah!" Before either of them could continue, a case was flying towards Madison's head until it hit her directly. The case of course was from Mandy.

"What the heck do you think you're doing?" Madison held her face, as the case did hit her pretty bad. It floated back over to Mandy and landed in her hand.

"Showing you who's the best."

"Why you-" Ms. Martinez teleported into the room, which caused a very small earthquake.

"Some of you guys may have been asking, what are you guys gonna learn this year?"

"If you were in my class 2 years ago, then you learned the basics of your instrument. How to play it, how to fight with it, and so on."

"If you were here last year, you would've learned how to use your powers to their very limit."

"This year, you'll learn how to do both. But, only on one condition." Ms. Martinez finished, so Madison decided to speak up.

"And what's that condition?" All of them were hit by some kind of beam, in which gave them some kind of uniform. The outfits had some circle on it. Most had an X in the circle, some had a slash through it, and few had no lines.

"You guys have to prove to me if you're the best of the best! Just remember that through these trials, you have to have your instrument by your side at all times." A box gracefully fell from the ceiling. Ms. Martinez picked it up and handed it to Madison.

"A gift that will help you get through the 2 Month Hero Trials." She placed it on the ground and began opening it, revealing an instrument case.

"A new Tenor?" Chloe asked, standing next to her. Madison got excited, so in spite of this, began opening the case. It was a new tenor, in fact, it was brand new also. Everything in side of it was wrapped up in plastic. It had some sort of aura come off of it, but it was welcoming to Madison, of course.

"This is the best day of my life!" She exclaimed, unwrapping the gold lacquer instrument. She thought it smelt like potato salad, but that didn't really matter to her.

In a random forest

"Ice Barrier!" A familiar voice shouted, sending a wave of ice towards the still unknown person. They deflected it away, and it covered the right side of the forest.

"All of you weaklings don't know what true power is." The mysterious person said, charging up dark energy. The familiar voice, who was now identified as Brandon, used an impact to shatter the ice.

"I've seen true power before, and it's Power!" Wind force from the Impact alone managed to make the figure step back a bit, not too much though.

"You're a lot stronger than the others." The figure pointed an arm towards him, and the cloak revealed a mechanical arm.

"But Sub-Legendaries aren't strong enough." A blast was fired from their hand, and collided with him, causing a large explosion.

Back in the band room

"Now, all we do is wait for the bras-" Ms. Martinez began, but soon interrupted by Allie kicking down the door.

"We're ready to go to the north pole!" She interrupted. Madison and the others were shocked by this information.

"What? The north pole?!"

Chapter 3

THE FIRST FIGHT

"I t's so cold down here..." Madison mumbled, even though she was stronger in the cold. Chloe would've responded, but she was completely frozen. Mandy was shivering too, but not too much. Ms. Martinez stood proud, like she was immune to this kind of weather.

"You'll get used to it. We'll be here for 4 months, remember?" She responded, and Madison nodded.

"First training. 2.0, fight Allie. Only setback is that you have to keep the tenor on your back."

"What?" Madison and Allie questioned, both confused. Ms. Martinez just gave them the signal to begin. Madison charged towards Allie, about to throw a punch. Before she did, she used a blast to knock herself backwards.

"I see what she's planning. I can't use attacks with too much movement, or else the tenor might get dented." She thought, just standing her ground. Allie used this opportunity to generate the energy from the band festival in her hand.

"Die!" She shouted, blasting it towards Madison. Madison knew she couldn't move much, so she pointed her hands to the center of the blast.

"Split!" When the blast came in contact with the tip of her finger, her reflexes kicked in, and she split the blast in two by separating her hands.

"Perfect coordination. It's the only way she can win without moving too much, but it drains her energy." Ms. Martinez thought, while they were still having their face off.

"Power-nade!" Madison clapped her hands together, then immediately after, used a blast to push Allie back. Allie blocked the attack, but it turned into smoke quickly after.

"Step it up a notch!" She exclaimed, using her hand to wipe away the smoke. Madison did so by teleporting behind her and using her superiority to constantly vanish over and over again. She did this until there were multiple mirages surrounding her.

"I wonder which one is real." One of them said, and Allie couldn't pinpoint which one it was. That's until the actual Madison started spinning in a circle, she was above Allie.

"Powerful Pistol!" Madison shouted, pointing one of her fingers towards Allie, and releasing a large amount of energy from it, compressed into a ball.

"Deflect!" Allie countered, using her one named attack to push it back towards Madison. Expecting this, she caught it with her hand and turned it into smoke. By just using her arm, she activated Drive 2.

"Alright, this is the final act!" Madison began charging a blast, which was similar to her 'Powerful Blaster'.

"It's..." She started, about to fire off the blast. Allie prepared herself by raising her arms to block.

"Looks like she has complete control over Drive 2. The uneven energy waves are gone, but steady now." Ms.

Martinez said, also anticipating this seemingly ultimate attack.

"Joke!" Instead of energy coming out, it was actually confetti. Allie dropped her guard.

"Are you serious?"

"Yes." Madison then started charging up some other kind of power up. It was similar to her shockwaves, but the lightning was the same color as Power.

"Hurry and wrap this up you two! We've got to make it to the building!" Ms. Martinez interjected, so Madison turned around to face her.

"Since when was there a building on th-" Allie saw this as an opportunity to take the win, so she charged towards her. Madison was completely oblivious to this. Allie punched her in the face, which knocked her on the ground.

"You lose!" Madison held her face while getting up, firing off mini blasts in her other hand.

"That was a cheap shot! Give me a rematch later."

"Shut up, 2.0." Ms. Martinez said, as Madison was being dragged by Mandy to wherever she was leading them too.

"Okay." Once they made it to the previously mentioned building, almost everyone was in shock. It was the two band houses, moved to the north pole. Madison, after being let go by Mandy, stood up in amazement.

"Hey! This is cool!" Ms. Martinez stood in front of the band house extended, where she lives.

"I moved it here all by myself! Let's gather in the original band house!" She ran inside, and Madison immediately followed her, then with everyone else. As everyone sat down, Madison stood up to say something.

"Alright guys, this is the new low reed roster! Of course, we have me as Tenor, and Chloe as the Bari." She began, pointing towards the shelves in the corner.

"We have Aaliyah and Bailey as our still Bass Clarinets like normal, isn't that somewhat cool?" Mandy had her arms crossed.

"Not really."

"Shut up, dishwasher. Anyway, since we're beginning our hero trials, it's only fair that the number one hero explains everything."

"Oh, yeah! The hero trials are when our professional heroes watch over you guys while we go through many tests. They pick out who could be their sidekicks until a few of you guys actually get your licenses." Ms. Martinez announced to everyone.

"They especially are looking for ones that are heroic, so you guys should step up your saving attitude. You too 2.0!"

"What? I've saved a lot of people. If it wasn't for me, Chloe would've killed all of you!"

"What if you were put in a situation where you weren't there for everyone? Even vice versa, you couldn't do much."

"Fine, I lose."

"Now, it's time for my favorite part after explaining something!" Ms. Martinez lifted her arm into the air.

"It's 'part in the story that's mainly looked over but has important details' time!"

Now in the Band House extended

Madison fell over a little bit but caught herself before Allie could notice. However, Mandy noticed this.

"You're a loser." She said, as Madison was walking by. She pointed at her, and then clapped her hands together, making a small blast.

"If you don't shut up, I'll send you to next Thursday." She countered, then sitting down. Chloe sat down next to her, as Mandy crossed her arms.

"Since all of us are the strongest, I'm guessing you guys all felt that large drop in power." Chloe stated, as Allie nodded.

"Of course, we did. Brandon gives off the same amount of energy that Madison does, but it doesn't have a villain tracker like she does." Allie responded, which made Madison frown.

"Shut up. You're not all that strong yourself."

"Madison, shut up." Walter interrupted, also in the same room. The other member of the Big Three, James, was in the room too.

"Okay, sorry. But anyway, about that other power level. Who could it be?" Madison questioned.

"It's obvious, stupid!" Mandy answered.

"Then who was it?"

"That mystery idiot that you tried to fight earlier." Chloe punched Mandy in the arm.

"I wouldn't call them an idiot. They aren't dumb, because they somehow beat Brandon, who could destroy the world easily." Allie was focused on playing Tenor Adventures, but still listening in.

"They aren't exactly smart, either. Who makes cell bars that Madison could easily split in half, not even at full power?" She asked, which made Walter nod.

"A stupid person." Madison and Walter said at the same time. Mandy pointed a flame towards the door that lead to outside.

"Who's there?" Ms. Martinez ran in, trying her hardest to catch her breath. She looked up to everyone else.

"That cloaked person thing is here!"

BRICK OF SOUND

Chapter 4

THE INVINCIBLE MYSTERY

"**B**ring it on!" Madison called out, charging towards the person that's still unknown. Ms. Martinez reached her hand out towards her.

"Stop making stupid ideas!" Mandy followed suite with this charge, powering up a new attack. Madison activated her drive 3, which generated the lightning.

"Mighty Fist!" She launched her energy packed punch towards the figure, but still missed this attack. As it was seemingly on purpose, she turned to Mandy and grinned. She clapped her hands together, which made a blinding light filled with flames.

"Solar Flare!" When the bright light faded, it revealed Mandy next to Madison, as they were on the opposite side of everyone else. Walter tried activating his time control on the figure, but they simply continued walking, not affected.

"We need some sort of plan." Madison mumbled,

and Mandy looked down at her.

"You're now saying that?" As Chloe thought it was her turn, she brought out the energy sword like it was nothing.

"Galaxy Ripple!" She slammed the sword in the ground, which made a crack in the ice. The crack charged towards the figure, but they ended up jumping in the air. They were stuck in the air for a while.

"It's almost like they aren't affected by gravity." Ms. Martinez thought, still not stepping in. Kendall activated his full phoenix form and charged towards the person, but they dodged it almost effortlessly.

"You're all weaklings." They stated, landing on the ground. When they did, an effect of gravity came down on almost everyone, except for Mandy. As Madison was being pinned to the ground, she managed to stand up a bit. Ms. Martinez did so too.

"It looks like I'm gonna have to permanently damage something." Madison thought, glancing down at her leg, moving her gaze to her arm. She looked back at the figure.

"I'll save you for later." They told Ms. Martinez, turning around to face Madison. Once they made eye contact, on reflexes, she used Burst in her leg. It was powerful enough to remove the gravity effect for a few seconds, but also launched her towards them. She charged a burst in her right arm, which ripped her sleeve of the new outfit.

"Outburst!" When her fist hit the stomach of the figure, they stumbled back a bit, yet not much. All they had to do was tap Madison, and that sent her flying back to where she originally was. They turned back to Ms. Martinez, who was in shock of their amazing endurance. Chloe was too, of course.

"It's now your turn." While they were not paying attention, Allie charged up some of the energy that she herself didn't know where it came from. She fired off a blast at the person, who took it head on. It didn't do much damage though, it just burned their cloak a bit.

"This is the first time that we can't do anything." Mandy said, even though not affected by the gravity. She couldn't move, as any movement would get her killed. So, for one of the first times ever, she had to swallow her pride. Madison used her remaining useful arm to try crawling towards them.

"...I can't lose...not like this." She quietly told herself, despite how useless the action was. Her glasses came off of her eyes, rendering her unable to see clearly.

"Madison. Give up. You can't do anything." Mandy told her, so Madison looked up to her with the remaining strength she had.

"I never give up." She managed to say, before turning to face the mystery person. Ms. Martinez was charging up a energy fist.

"No one kills any one of my students!" She exclaimed, grabbing them by the shoulder. She decked them straight across the face, and they were actually hurt by this. Not by the sun energy, but by the pure strength of it.

"Come on, I just gotta get up and fight...!" Walter called out, fighting against the gravity pinning him down. The cloaked figure turned back to Madison, as the cloak itself was falling off from the punch. They finally were going to be revealed who the person was.

"Every single one of you I've killed in the future. Except for you." The still mysterious person said, looking down on Madison.

"Why's that?" Chloe asked her. They took off their cloak themselves, revealing an older Madison, with a mechanical arm. They looked about a few years older than her, and a bit taller.

"...what?" The Earthland Madison quietly questioned, as the future Madison began charging a blast from the before mentioned arm.

"I'm supposed to be the only one!" Future Madison shouted, firing off the blast. None of them could move, except for one person. The one person Madison didn't want to be hit. Mandy jumped in front of her, taking the blast at full force.

"That idiot." She thought, still being hit. Madison narrowed her eyes, not being able to see with her glasses knocked off. Once the blast finally finished, it revealed Mandy still standing. But one thing was missing. Her arm.

"Mandy! What the heck?" Madison tried getting up, still weak from breaking her arm. She ran towards Mandy with all of her energy and caught her when she fell.

"I can't let you d-" She began but was cut off by passing out. Ms. Martinez decided to guard them. The gravity effect was taken off, so the people still affected got up.

"Amy, it's fight together or die together." Alex told Amy, who was charging towards Future Madison. She looked back at him.

"120% Short Ranged Shot!" She cried out, firing off a large explosion towards her. Amy turned back to give an answer to Alex.

"We're fighting together to send her back to where she came from!" Amy finished, then turning back to stall Future Madison. Walter shattered the ice with his hands, which sent out a shockwave. An air portal began opening up, so everyone took this as an opportunity.

"Aside from her robot arm, everything else is bandaged. This means that if I can get close enough, I can send her flying." Allie told Chloe, who was charging her remaining energy into her sword.

"I can try backing you up, but it probably wouldn't

work." Chloe sent one of her flying slashes towards Future Madison, who jumped out of the way to dodge. When Allie found the time to be right, she charged towards her.

"You lose!" She kicked her straight in the stomach. This knocked the wind out of her, and also sent her flying towards the portal. Ms. Martinez teleported in front of the portal, charging a blast.

"This is what you get for messing with us!" Ms. Martinez shot the blast towards her, which sent her crashing into the portal. Walter closed it almost immediately, but then was drained out of his energy for keeping up such a big portal.

"Come on, Mandy. Get up..." Madison was still processing the situation, trying to shake her awake. She wouldn't be getting up anytime soon.

"I got her, 2.0." Ms. Martinez landed on the ground and picked up Mandy from Madison's arms.

"Thanks, mom."

BRICK OF SOUND

Chapter 5

OUT OF COMMISSION

"I can't believe this all just happened." Madison said to herself, looking up at the ceiling. She was now in her bed, laying down.

"Madison, go to bed." Allie told her from next door. Their rooms for both fortunately and unfortunately next to each other.

"I can't sleep."

"Do you want me to tell you a bedtime story?"

"No way."

"Then tell me what's on your mind." Madison sighed, looking over to one of the posters hung up on her wall.

"Mandy, of course. Are you stupid?"

"You're the stupid one, didn't you know that Ms. Martinez has some form of healing powers?"

"Can she heal a missing arm?"

"No one knows." Madison shifted her position on the bed to face the door.

"I mean, normally I could just sleep the pain off. But she kind of has Ms. Martinez's problem." She said.

"What's her problem?"

"Back when she destroyed Epitomus, the entire attack over exerted her body. Now she can't go max power for more than 5 minutes. In a place like the future, you always have to be at your best."

"I guess it really be like that sometimes." Madison laughed a little, but then going back to her usual inexpressive face.

"Shut up."

"Serious question. Did you forget what you told me on the way to Epitomus?"

"I said something like, 'Madison never gives up', right?"

"Yeah, so try taking your own advice." Before Madison could respond, she suddenly fell asleep. This was Allie's doing, as it was one of her new techniques.

The next day, after waking up, Madison went downstairs to try talking to Ms. Martinez. She walked up to her office, then opening the door.

"Ms. Martinez, how much longer will it be?" She questioned, peeking through the doorway.

"The blast had so much weird energy packed into it. It altered something with her power." Ms. Martinez answered, which made Madison remember something.

"You've probably found Brandon, right? What happened to him?"

"The blast took his arm as well, on the opposite side. On that same side, his hair changed color. Oddly, his body temperature went back to how it usually was."

"That's weird. How long will it be for them to wake up?"

"2 weeks, at maximum. We're gonna let Brandon stay

in the Band House extended until our trials are finished."

"Okay, see you later, mom."

"Don't call me that." Madison ran to the door, then opening it. She dashed outside, getting ready to do some practice.

"Alright, first order of business." She clapped her hands together, and immediately fired off a blast in front of her. It turned into smoke, like it usually would. Chloe walked out the door and patted her on the back.

"You've definitely improved, bro! Not as much as me, though." She told her, which made Madison smile.

"I'm pretty sure that the King of the Sky themselves wouldn't be able to get me on the ground, bro! Now, onto our plans." They both sat down on the ice, about to discuss something.

"Any new ideas may have to wait for some time, after recent events. There's also that mini side mission that you're doing." Madison nodded in approvement to this.

"Sure, we can wait. All we can do right now is hope for the best."

Near the spaceship

"Okay guys, we're setting sail for the future!" EP Madison exclaimed, with her arms crossed. She had a pirate hat on her head, which gave her some form of pride somehow.

"How're we supposed to get there?" EP Mandy questioned, as EP Madison kept her same expression.

"No clue!"

BRICK OF SOUND

Back in the North Pole

"I need to come up with a new gadget." Kendall said, holding his hammer with both hands.

"Maybe something like…" He took off his Tenor Detector and placed it on his worktable. He began hammering it, trying to change it into something else. In another room, Brandon and Mandy would be sleeping.

"I hate you." Brandon mumbled, but then going back to sleep.

"I hate you too." Mandy responded, then going to sleep also. Ms. Martinez watched this happen, before walking out the door.

"Looks like they're back to normal." Madison walked up to her room, about to take a nap. When she opened her door, it revealed Allie looking for something.

"What is it this time, idiot?" Madison asked sarcastically, earning a look from Allie.

"I'm looking for 'Orange Juice Recipes'." She replied, then continuing her search. Madison threw it at her head, which caught her by surprise.

"There. Now, get out of my room!" Allie picked it up off the floor and made her way to the door.

"I'll bring it back to you in a few days."

"Whatever." Madison laid down on her bed, attempting to go to sleep. She brought her broken hand up to her face.

"It's gonna take me a whole day or two of sleep to heal this a little." Madison put her arm down back to her side.

"Allie! Put me to sleep!" She shouted to her, while she was in her own room, reading through the notebook.

"Don't need to tell me twice!" Madison instantly went asleep, probably waking up unless some other interference wakes her up. Chloe was in the room below her, looking at her Bari case.

"Looks like the old one is going to be staying here."

BRICK OF SOUND

"Even though I knew they could survive, I shouldn't have used up all of that energy into a punch." Ms. Martinez stated, as smoke came out of her mouth.

"I have to try steadying my power level, since it's unst-" Before she could finish, Kendall opened the door, holding the upgraded Tenor Detector in his hand.

"I've got just the thing for you, 'big M'!" He tossed it over to her, and she caught it easily and put it on.

"What is it, exactly?"

"It stops your power from dramatically decreasing, of course! The only downside is that large scaled attacks can drop it!"

"Thanks, bassoon." Kendall gave her a thumbs up.

"Anything to keep the number one hero as number one!" In the other room, Brandon began waking up. He stepped out of the bed.

"This isn't the forest. Where am I?" He looked at himself in the mirror, noticing that the tips of his hair were completely white. He also noticed that his right arm was covered in ice.

"She's probably going to think I look like an old man." Brandon said, looking back at Mandy.

"That weakling." He got up and walked out of the door, trying to find out where he was.

"Looks like you're awake." Chloe said, outside of the room. Brandon glanced at her.

"Shut up, King of Losers!"

"No you, Ice Cream Truck!" After staring each other down for a few minutes, they directed their attention the opposite way.

"If I got the chance, I would defeat you." Chloe stated.

"I'd like to see you try; cause I'm going to become the top hero!" Brandon claimed, pointing at his frozen arm.

"The curse has been pretty handy in saving my own life."

"That's because curse users can't die without it being removed first." Before they could continue arguing, Ms. Martinez showed up.

"Can't believe you've already woken up. You must have some awesome endurance." She told Brandon, which gave him a sense of pride.

"Of course I do, I'm going to become the top hero!" He crossed his arms, making Chloe a little mad.

"Not unless I do it first!" Allie came downstairs, angry from all of the yelling.

"No, I'm going to be the top hero!" Ms. Martinez walked back to her office, as they were still arguing with each other.

"So much for peace." Madison was still sleeping, until suddenly waking up. She sat up in her bed.

"That dream was not enjoyable in the slightest." Using her advanced hearing, Chloe heard this and ran up to her room.

"You're coming with me, bro."

"Wha-" Before she could question this, Chloe dragged her down to where the 3 of them were still arguing.

"You see this right here? This is number one hero material!" Madison brought her now scared arm up to her forehead in a salute.

"Full Speed Ahead!" Allie and Brandon both looked at Madison.

"Which one of us is stronger?" They questioned her at the same time, which made Madison think for a second.

"It's almost a complete tie except in endurance and destructive capability, making Brandon a little worse in those categories." Chloe nodded in agreement, letting go of Madison.

"You can go back to your Power Nap now, bro!" She joked, which made Madison laugh as she went back upstairs.

"Alright, see you guys later." Brandon went outside of the Band House Extended and felt how cold it was.

"Looks like a good spot to train." He took off his large jacket that was almost completely destroyed by the blast from Future Madison and threw it at the ground.

"Ice Breaker!" He exclaimed, placing his hand on the cold ice. The ice from his curse came out, but it was a darker shade of blue than regular ice now, yet not by much. He turned his hand on the ice into a fist, which shattered it completely.

"That's weird." Mandy finally woke up.

"Where is that bast-" She shouted, then looking at herself in the mirror. Her arm that was damaged had been replaced but was still bandaged. She got up and headed outside to where Brandon was.

"Well look who's awake." Brandon said, about to use one of his ice attacks. Mandy was shocked as to why he was here.

"You look like an old man." Mandy retaliated, which gave him a dead panned expression.

"Knew it." He thought. Madison couldn't go to sleep, so she stared up at the ceiling with her arms crossed.

"Sleep time." She said, closing her eyes. She almost went to sleep but opened her eyes again.

"Nevermind." Allie walked in Madison's room, holding 'Orange Juice Recipes'.

"I'll hand you this back tonight. I'm almost done with it." Madison threw a pen at her.

"If you want to, you can add something." Allie caught it and left the room. Madison shifted her position, and finally went to sleep.

Chapter 7

BETTER UPGRADES

"**A**lright, winter outfits time!" Madison exclaimed, pointing up to the ceiling of the bottom floor. Her outfit was a black shirt with black jeans, with the new addition of a blue utility belt. Her shoes had tough armor on them, maybe made out of iron.

"You're just going to freeze to death." Mandy responded. Her outfit wasn't really different, except her vest was replaced with a jacket. The Blazing Blasters, the gauntlets made by Kendall, were changed from the white color to black.

"I'm stronger in the cold, so jokes on you!" Allie punched her in the face before she could say anything else. Allie's outfit wasn't much different from Mandy's, but she didn't have oversized gloves like she did. In turn, her jacket was oversized. Madison used one of her iron shoes to kick Allie across the face.

"Yeah, but are you stronger in the sky?" Chloe interrupted. Her outfit was almost the same as her regular hero outfit, but the cape in a lot longer, as in it goes around her body.

"By a small number, yes, but I'm still cooler than you, not Section Leader! I even have proof!" Since it's been two months since they were attacked, Madison showed her the results from their chair tests. She pointed at her name, which was at the top of the low reed section.

"I'm way cooler than you!" Chloe retaliated, but before they could continue, Ms. Martinez came out of her office.

"Come on guys, we have to make it back to the school to get your results!" Almost immediately after, Madison hopped on the tenor case, and bolted out of the door.

"Let's go, saxophone salad!" She exclaimed, flying away into the air. She sat down on the instrument, holding onto it so she doesn't fall off.

"I wonder if I passed the hero trials."

Flashback Begin

"PC Bullet!" Madison called out, concentrating Power into the center of her palm. A compressed beam shot out, breaking through a few chunks of ice.

"What does PC stand for?" Allie asked her, as smoke came out of Madison's hand.

"Power Concentrated, stupid. I had to shorten it down."

"Well how was I supposed to know that?"

"Using context clues."

Flashback End

Madison sighed, laying down on her tenor case, still keeping her grip on it so she doesn't fall off.

"If only I could succeed at something." She said, as the instrument blasted through the sky. She lost her ability to fly after leaving sky island, and so she thinks it was a one-time occurrence.

"Too bad, I guess it's just gonna be the two of us forever." Madison grinned, patting the top part of the case. It glowed green, showing a form of enjoyment of this statement.

"That's of course unless I get you a little friend." While she shot towards her destination, Ms. Martinez and everyone else arrived at the school by her teleportation.

"2.0 is probably going to be arrive after us, so let's wait a bit." Ms. Martinez told everyone. When Madison showed up where they were, she grabbed the handle of her tenor and floated down to the ground.

"You're late." Mandy blatantly stated, earning a look from Madison, who didn't really care.

"Not really." Ms. Martinez got an idea from this.

"Since we have around 1 hour until we have to go in, how about I pick the two who fought in the beginning to do a quick sparring match with me?" She said.

"Heck yeah!" Allie exclaimed as a response. Madison agreed, but didn't say anything.

"Okay, you guys can begin whenever you want." Ms. Martinez claimed, and Allie charged towards her with slightly improved speed.

"Looks like we have the same idea!" Madison began charging a concentrated blast in her left palm. Ms. Martinez dodged Allie's random punching and kicking that had no pattern in it.

"That's the will to fight. Her attacks aren't in any order, but all of them are trying to land that one lucky shot." She thought. Right when Allie thought she landed a hit; Ms. Martinez used a blast to dodge upwards.

"What?!" Allie ducked, knowing that Madison had finished her attack. She fired the blast at Ms. Martinez, who deflected it out of the way. All of the things in its path were left with a hole in it. The power of the blast damaged her hand a little bit, but not by a lot.

"My turn!" Madison used her also improved speed to launch herself towards Ms. Martinez, and Allie jumped out of the way. She clapped her hands together, trying to use a fake diversion.

"Power Breach!" Ms. Martinez covered her eyes with her arm, expecting the smoke attack. But instead, Madison kicked her upwards into the air.

"Get ready to d-" Allie appeared above her, doing some form of sledgehammer attack, only to be interrupted by Ms. Martinez blinding her with a little of her raw sun energy.

"Be more careful, stupid!" Madison activated Drive 2 to teleport behind Ms. Martinez. She used the same technique she used against Allie, the one where she makes multiple mirages of herself to confuse the enemy.

"To protect the other, you guys are trading places. That's a decent strategy." Ms. Martinez fired off a blast and controlled the direction of it to hit all of the distractions. The real Madison blocked the attack, which pushed her back until the blast disappeared.

"But it's too mediocre!" Madison clapped her hands together, channeling up the 345 energy. The lines were all the same as the last time she used it, but once it reached her eyes, her right one changed color. It changed to the color of the curse's energy.

"I'm the coolest one around, the number one! No

one's going to take me down!" Allie regained her senses, charging the unknown energy again. Ms. Martinez noticed something about this energy.

"It gives off something similar to a curse, but it really isn't. Maybe it's superiority cu-" Before she could finish her thoughts, Madison charged up a blast with both of her hands at once. Once she got ready to block the attack, Madison teleported in front of her.

"Instant Blast!" She exclaimed, firing off the blast, which set off an immediate explosion. When the smoke cleared, it revealed Ms. Martinez guarding the attack, but using her sun energy to help her. Madison looked at Allie and grinned.

"Loser." Ms. Martinez blew some of the smoke away that was coming off of her arms.

"Not bad. You still have some things to improve on. Let's head into the school."

———————————

A figure was walking around, obviously not on Earth. It seemed like they were looking for something. They came across a large gold cube, completely towering them in size. There was writing in it, but in another language.

"Ah, so this is the thing he was researching! A race in space, huh." They thought, surprised by it actually being there. By looking at them observing the block, one could tell they were able to read what was written.

"...Prophecies do become a lot frequent these days, might as well believe it. Don't know when or who, though."

BRICK OF SOUND

NEW MENTORS

After a few weeks, everyone was assigned a mentor. It was now the month of October, which Madison was hyped for due to 8th Grade Night. But before she could do that, she had to meet her new teacher. She opened the door to the cleared-out classroom.

"Hi Señora S-" She began but couldn't see her anywhere. Madison set her bookbag down and was later greeted by a swift kick to her face.

"Always keep your guard up at all times!" The now revealed Señora Salcedo told her, which made Madison nod. She dusted off her pants.

"You're too fast for me, I can't even sense your energy most of the time!"

"Then you have to catch up with me. Simple!" She darted around the room very fast, making Madison raise her arms to block. Once she felt something touch her back, she immediately turned around to blast it. Of course, nothing was there. Madison was kicked in the back, sending her flying until hitting the wall face first.

"That's one of your flaws. Your instant response time will eventually lead to your downfall."

Outside the Band Room

"Do it one more time!" Ms. Martinez called out, as Chloe yelled while firing off a large blast. She almost fell over from exhaustion, but she had to keep standing. The Bari that was on her would be dented from this, and it's already in bad condition.

"Because of how strong you are, you're used to having short battles. You have to be trained to exert many amounts of energy! Now, come at me!" Chloe ran towards her with the remaining strength she had left and threw a punch at her. Ms. Martinez dodged the punch, which made Chloe turn around with her last burst of energy. She managed to land a punch on her face but didn't make her even flinch. She fired off a small blast from this hand, which acted as a stun type attack.

"Too much." Chloe said, taking the harness off. She fell over on the ground but wasn't knocked out.

"Looks like you need a break." Ms. Martinez offered her hand to her, but she shook her head in response.

"No way. The Bari never gives up." Chloe answered, trying to get up but ultimately failing. Ms. Martinez helped her up.

"Even heroes need breaks sometimes. Where do you want to go?"

CHAPTER 8: NEW MENTORS

Near the Band Houses

James had to teach the Kelli Squad about fighting more efficiently. Since he knew about the majority of their powers, he could help them out. Walter tried to learn from him also, as much as he could.

"If you guys want to be heroes, you're going to have at least the basics of combat strength." He explained to them.

"I don't want to be a hero." Kandi responded.

"Not to sound rude, but why are you here then? All of us are training to become heroes." Elizabeth asked her, tone not matching with words.

"It just sounds like a lot of work, that's all. Plus, some of them are just weird." She elaborated on her reasoning.

"Either way, you have to defend yourself in this world." Aaliyah told her, as Walter nodded in agreement.

"Well, that settles it! Let's get stronger!" Kelli exclaimed.

Some Island in Space

"Everyone else has regular training, but I have to train by screaming." Allie mumbled, floating from the gravitational force.

"Step up your game! The people on Earth have to be able to hear you!" Her mentor, Ms. Stevens, who just so happened to have the Legendary power Moon, exclaimed. It gave her the ability to breathe in space, with other advanced combat abilities. She was the number 3 hero, right below Señora Salcedo. Her power was Stealth, Sub-Legendary to Power.

"Why can't I just practice something else?"

"Because you don't know anything else! You've mastered your power, so you have to do the smaller things to get to the big ones!"

"Can you at least show me a glimpse of how strong you are?" Allie questioned, as Ms. Stevens motioned her to move out of the way. She moved at least a few feet away from the island.

"Island Wiper!" She charged a blast from her mouth and fired it at the island, which blew it up. It was completely decimated, which left Allie in shock while floating in space.

"Oh."

Somewhere not too far from the school

"Since you're so strong apparently, I want you to blast me with all you got." Mrs. Staller told Mandy, who complied with charging a flame attack with both hands.

"Alpha Black Fire!" The blast used against Brandon in the Band Festival was used, and Mrs. Staller simply shot a bullet through it, splitting the blast in half, going different directions.

"You call that a blast? That wasn't good enough! Try harder!"

"Her bullets are made out of some other worldly metal that can go through anything. That's not even her full power either." Mandy thought, charging another one. Once it was fired, Mrs. Staller shot another bullet through it again, this time making it explode.

"That was one of my explosive rounds. Each shot has a random chance of being any type of my bullets, including the piercing one. So, I'd be more careful if I were you."

CHAPTER 8: NEW MENTORS

Back in the classroom

"Just remember this, your power is chosen like some sort of spinning wheel. It's a very large one, yet you were still born powerless by the smallest chance. That is some bad luck." Señora Salcedo stated.

"It was either that or some horrible common. I think the wheel made a great choice." Madison responded, wrapping bandages around her head.

"Horrible or not, being powerless isn't a good thing. The chances weren't in your favor, and you probably received bad treatment because of it."

"Well, I'm not powerless anymore. They gave me the best power around, and that wasn't for a bad reason! I just can't pass it down anymore, so I'm the last one."

"That's too bad. But, hopefully you'll learn something new while out in space. See you later."

"Of course!" Madison picked up her bag and ran off, so she can get some sort of head start on the way back to the band house.

"Everyone is one step ahead in different factors than me, but I'm still the cooler one." She thought, making herself smile.

"Let's see how far I can get this time."

BRICK OF SOUND

Chapter 9

A RACE IN SPACE

Of course, before they go to space, they have to set up the spaceship. But there's one thing missing, or technically multiple. The Epitomus people were gone.

"Did they tell you they were leaving?" Chloe asked Ms. Martinez, who shook her head.

"No. Maybe they were in some sort of rush...?" She answered, and Madison walked in between them and straight into the ship.

"Well, that wouldn't make sense. Epitomus Madison would've just randomly appeared to tell us!" Madison said, which made Chloe think.

"You aren't wrong." She responded. Ms. Martinez got an idea.

"We're going to take more than just a few people on this trip! Kendall, go and rebuild the ship!" She called out to him, and he landed on top of the ship and got out his toolkit.

"Say no more!" After around 5 minutes, the ship was

completely renovated. It was much bigger, and somehow had more rooms than it usually did. The rooms were greater in size also.

"Do I get my own room?" Madison questioned him, and he jumped down to the entrance.

"To save space, I combined some of the rooms. You have to share a room!" Madison wasn't fazed by this, not showing much emotion.

"Okay." Sometime after this new update, everyone got settled in either the living room or their respective rooms.

"Why are we going to space exactly?" Chloe asked Ms. Martinez.

"It's a quest to find information on this other species that was on some planet but was later destroyed. According to our records, there's one left. They're a part of the royal family."

"That's cool." Madison said.

"That's stupid. Who would destroy an entire planet just out of the blue?" Bailey, one of the bass clarinets, interjected.

"Probably you." Chloe retaliated, earning an agreement from Madison.

"Shut up, Madison."

"I didn't do anything!" The ship hit something, and it was obviously not on track for a target. The door from the entrance was opened, and it was of course the one mentioned came in.

"Why the heck did you hit me?!" She exclaimed.

"We're supposed to keep this book PG, shut up!" Madison responded.

"Fine." Allie crossed her arms and sat down in the closest seat to her.

"What was this race called?" Madison brought back up.

"Demon. They were a race of demons." Ms. Martinez answered.

"That's great. Another practically dead race, probably not deserving it's destruction." Mandy said, coming out of her room.

"They were cold blooded killers, filled with rage. Just going to say that the person who destroyed it wasn't too far from that themselves."

"But still, it wasn't deserved. Whoever the last survivor is probably won't be able to deal with the news." Madison stated, earning a nod from Chloe.

"Maybe you're the demon princess." Mandy retaliated.

"No chance." She got up and headed to her room, not looking forward to any future conversations.

"We aren't too far from our first destination, so I guess I'll take a little nap." She closed her eyes, and soon fell asleep, despite usually never being able to sleep easily. In her dreams, it seemed to be Future Madison indirectly showing her the vision. Where it took place was unknown to her. She sensed it might be important, though.

It wasn't that major, but she saw two blobs shaped like people in front of her. One was taller than the other, colored as pink, and the other was blue.

"...They don't need to know that we're here!" The blue one said in a hushed whisper.

"Sorry, it's because of Joe." Pink responded. The other figure's body language showed that it was visibly confused.

"...Who's Joe?" Pink held back as best as she could.

"Joe Mama!"

...

...How was this important, exactly?

Madison woke up, got off of her bed and made her way to the entrance of the ship.

"Because I just so happen to have the Sun power, all of you guys can breathe in space. As long as my energy can reach you." Ms. Martinez explained, stepping foot onto the moon.

"Epic!" Madison ran outside and ended up tripping over herself. She began floating, fortunately for her not to fall and slam her face on something again.

"What an idiot." Allie said to her, having complete control on her gravitational force. All of the ones with Mythical powers were hardly able to walk but got help from everyone else. The ones with Sun Sub-Legendaries ended up similar to them, but due to Ms. Martinez's presence, were able to get around.

"Even more luck from you, luck jackpot. Your realm of being stronger just so happens to be space." Madison responded, spinning upside down.

"Guess that makes me the King of Space!"

"More like King of G-"

"Madison, shut up." Walter interjected before Madison could continue. She did stop talking, but probably not for long.

"Hey, where did Ms. Martinez go?" Chloe asked, as the one in question was missing.

"On the other side of the moon, I guess." Amy answered. She in fact was right, as Ms. Martinez somehow got lost not even 5 minutes after leaving the spaceship.

"That's weird. Everyone must have gotten lost." She said, walking around to find her way back. Instead, she was greeted by a large stone engravement. It was in gold, holding some form of value, and the writing was in a different language.

"Holy bowl of cereal."

Chapter 10

TRUE ROYALTY

"So, this is what you found, mom." Madison told Ms. Martinez, who nodded. Allie crossed her arms and walked up to the valuable writing.

"It obviously says 'The Oni Royalty must be kept alive, no matter the cost. Our king has to rule over us during this battle, so we can truly defeat the humans.' I don't know why you can't read that." Everyone stared at her, not thinking that this would happen.

"What? Stop looking at me!"

"Wow. You're actually this stupid." Madison dumbfoundedly said. She wasn't in denial but didn't really believe it.

"Unbelievable." Ms. Martinez stated, amazed by this new information. Allie still wasn't aware of what was going on.

"What's the problem?"

"It's obvious that you're the princess of the demon clan." They answered at the same time, and she just stood there for a few seconds.

"Meaning that your real last name is Oni, which translates into demon. Your first name probably isn't your actual name either." Chloe continued, leaning on the side of the stone.

"I'm the what?!"

Around an hour later

"What is a python thermal?" Madison questioned, floating upside down again.

"It's Pythagorean Theorem. Something related to math. I wouldn't know." Ms. Martinez answered.

"No one needed to know that, Madison." Bailey responded.

"This is why Madison should be banned." Aaliyah said, making Madison shake her head.

"No way, you're the guys that should've been banned a long time ago! Especially the original low reeds. You guys threw me into a forest, and I was stuck there for a week!"

"That seems like a personal problem." Walter interjected, gaining the agreement from 2 out of 3 of the bass clarinets.

"Since this is more of a research trip, there's not much for us to do except for going to different islands. Besides, we can't stay here for too long because we might find some information that we don't need to know." Chloe reminded everyone else.

"If we found more info on the Space War, we'd definitely get in trouble with the government. It's just known as a war in space, not giving any other details." Ms. Martinez stated.

"So why don't we leave?" Madison asked, now flipped sideways by Mandy.

"We can't. We still need to explore. So, treat this as some sort of vacation." Chloe answered, which made her nod.

In the future

"Losers." Future Madison said, sitting on a nearby rock. Blood came down her face, but that was the only injury she received. Everyone from Epitomus, including EP Madison, were just lying there behind her. They were beaten up, possibly even dead.

"Now there's only 1 person left." She held her mechanical arm, that was barely phased.

"That number one hero that almost took my life twice."

On a nearby island

"Madison." A voice ominously said, gaining the attention of her. Madison recognized her as Chloe, but older than the one she knows.

"Yes?" Chloe extended her hand to her.

"You have our trust." Madison, surprised by this, reached her hand out to meet the other. But before she could touch it, she vanished into thin air, just leaving her there.

"Must've been a vision." She looked around for anything significant, so she can have an excuse to make herself seem useful.

"Okay. Let's see what this is." She found some weird

metal, close to the color of Alex's steel. Madison crushed it in her right hand, and nothing happened.

"Great." She thought, then returning to the ship via flying. When she made it inside, she went into her room.

"How am I a demon?" Allie questioned herself, standing on her bed while looking through Orange Juice Recipes.

"You're probably not even full demon. They actually look demonic, and you look like a human. So maybe you're half...?" Madison said, walking over and sitting on her bed.

"But I can't be royalty!" She exclaimed, still not gaining full interest from Madison.

"Too bad, you are. You should be glad about being royalty, cause that makes you a few steps above everyone else in becoming the number one hero."

"So, I'm a few steps above you?"

"No way! I'm ahead of everyone else cause of my power!"

"But don't you think that isn't fair?" Madison didn't pay mind to this, because this is another thing related to her due to circumstances.

"It's just pure luck. It's the only thing I'm good at. Sure, I am special, but I can't just win normally. Technically, I've always lost my battles."

"Does that mean I'm your only win?"

"Stop asking so many questions. I'm going to bed." Allie took this as a yes, so she stopped standing on the bed.

"Remember we have another adventure tomorrow!" Ms. Martinez shouted from her office.

"No." Madison then shut her eyes, eventually going to sleep despite not usually able to, meaning something important was going to be told to her. When she opened her eyes, she was submerged underwater.

"I wonder if I can create a light to see." She thought, putting her hands close to each other. A small blast was generated by her, and began moving downwards, since that was the only thing she knew how to do. Eventually, every time she moved down, something very bright began glowing. She stopped using the energy and continued towards this light.

"Oh. A flame under water? Cool!" She tried to grab it, but it just moved further down. Somewhat mad by this, she kept on chasing after it, trying to catch it, but not succeeding. Madison went out of her way to use some of her energy to chase it, still unable to reach it.

"I see what you're trying to say to me. You could've just said it up front!" In realization of what was going on, she still ran after this fire, but eventually hitting the floor of this body of water. The flame simply passed through this floor and was very close to Madison. But due to how strong this barrier was, she couldn't get through it. She sighed, giving up on this attempt.

"Guess the prophecy was right."

Flashback Begin

"The prophecy of the one with the last. It's talked about in this book." EP Allie told the two Madison's, holding up the 345 book.

"What does it say?" Madison asked, as 345 Madison already knew what it was about.

"The prophecy reads, 'The one who's never succeeded, always strives to. The one who's never succeeded, chases after many goals, but never prevails. The one goal that is seen to be in view is never achieved but is still followed. But, like always, the one who's never succeed, was never close.'"

"That doesn't have anything to do with me right now." Madison crossed her arms but was soon sent upwards back into the real world.

"Then prepare yourself, true hero. For the never-ending taunts from life and death themselves!"

Madison awoke in another dream, glad to be away from the last one. She was in front of another one of those gold blocks with writing inscribed in them.

"'Fates shall collide with the one and the king, and it shall be over for humans. If we lose this war, then that will be our final turning point.'" She read. Her usual neutral demeanor turned into that of confusion.

"...the one?"

"**N**o, I will not wake up." Madison mumbled, falling off the bed. Drive 2 was activated in her sleep.

"If you don't wake up, I'll throw you out with the rest of the alto trash!" Allie shouted, kicking her into a wall. This woke her up, and disabled Drive 2.

"I'm tenor trash, not alto trash! Get it right, idiot!" Before Madison could properly stand up, Allie threw her at the door, making her crash through it.

"Great timing, 'Stupid Tenor'. We're just about to lea-" Mandy began, interrupted by seeing Madison on the ground.

"I did what you asked, now leave me alone." Allie said, picking up Madison and carrying her.

"Wait, you're the one who planned this entire thing?" She asked Mandy, then having tape put over her mouth by Ash.

"Now we can have a peaceful adventure." Madison

wasn't mad at this, so went along with it. At the beginning of the adventure, everything went fine. That's until they made it to a specific island. Right when Madison was on the island, a book appeared above her head. It fell on top of her, knocking her out of the hold of Allie.

"Nice." She told herself from under the tape and picked it up to look at it. On the front, it was revealed as one of the book of curses, the one about 345.

"Toss me that, 2.0." Ms. Martinez said to her, in which Madison complied. She caught it and went straight to reading it. Allie ripped the tape off of her face, causing her to punch her in the arm as a reflex. This was a bad move, as Allie blasted her in the face, at the same time as Madison.

"What is this?" Kelli questioned, looking at the book through her goggles. There was invisible writing on the dusty cover.

"It says something like, 'Your Epitomus friends are in the future'." Madison answered, while being blasted by Allie.

"Everything seems to be normal in the book. Except for one thing. This prophecy." Ms. Martinez stated.

"Wait! No! Don't look at that!" Madison exclaimed, quickly activating Drive 2 to grab the book and move out the way in the fraction of a second.

"Oh. It's the prophecy of the last. Big deal, all of the top pros already know what it is." Ms. Martinez retaliated, as the book magically appeared in her hand.

"The book is older than everyone here. Well, almost everyone." Chloe said, then looking at Bailey.

"I'm not old. You're just jealous cause your power sucks." The two got neck and neck, but Madison stepped in between them, knocking Chloe back.

"You're one to talk, coming from someone who can only create light!" She countered.

"All you can do is fight people weaker than you and

lose! Anyone who's actually stronger than you, someone like me, would beat you up!" When Madison took the first chance to fire a blast, Ms. Martinez threw the book at her.

"Oops. My fingers slipped."

"That was completely intentional!"

Flashback Begin

"Night Light!" Bailey exclaimed, upper cutting Madison from under her chin. While it stung a little, she recovered fast enough after.

"Power Hammer!" Madison used a sledgehammer like attack to return to her. They were on the hero trials, a few days, maybe a week or two, before they went back to the school.

"It only took a few months for her to start a little rivalry. That's…" Ms. Martinez began, watching this practice sparring match.

"…impressive."

Flashback End

"There shouldn't be many fights on this adventure, and if I catch any of you guys doing anything like that, consider yourself kicked out!" Ms. Martinez yelled, obviously serious.

"That's the third time she's said that." Madison whispered to her friend Kim, another clarinet, and they both laughed.

"Chloe, I want you to keep patrol at night and make sure that Madison doesn't do anything weird."

"What? I don't do anything weird. That's Allie's fault!"

"No, that's her fault!" While the two were arguing, Chloe nodded at this form of superiority, something she didn't have, but did in different ways.

"Okay. I can do that." Madison was thrown at the spaceship, slammed into it, and began floating around the gravitational pull. Everyone returned to the ship, with Chloe grabbing onto Madison and bringing her back to them, of course being upside down.

"We'll be returning the day before 8th grade night, which is two days from now. Be prepared!" Ms. Martinez announced to everyone.

"How do you think Bailey was accepted into the low reeds?" Madison asked in a whisper to Kim.

"She probably beat up a lot of kids." She answered, and the both of them laughed again.

"I can make you blind right now." Bailey told Madison specifically, not in any interest.

"Do it then!" Before the former mentioned could do so, Madison was thrown by Allie again into the room.

"Wouldn't it be bad if a villain were to just show up?" Allie hypothetically asked, as a figure landed onto the moon silently behind them.

"That would be pretty bad, yes." They said, gaining the attention of everyone that was outside of the spaceship. It was Future Madison, with her cloak back.

"What do you want from us?" Mandy asked her, about to blast her.

"Meet me down at sky island." She vanished into thin air, leaving the group there.

"Jeez Allie, you gave us bad luck." Walter said, as Allie stormed into the spaceship.

"We're going down there now to kick her a-"

"Woah, keep it PG!" Madison shouted from the room, which didn't shut her up.

CHAPTER 11: RETURN

Down at Caelum Insula

On a separate island near the actual one, Future Madison sat down near a sanctuary.

"Looks like the small one has the thing I've been wanting for a while. A following." She thought, looking at a power crystal shard on a stand.

"Maybe I could see if the Land Beyond could grant me a wish. I'm pretty sure they'll let me go for my actions, since that's the way the timeline designed me." Future Madison stood up, and right after, the ship previously on the moon around 10 minutes later crashed down next to the deserted city on the other island. The door to it opened, but before Future Madison could even blink, Allie appeared right in front of her.

"The demon princess is here to beat me up?" She taunted, then being punched across the face. Future Madison was knocked back a bit by this, and obviously hurt from it.

"I am not the demon princess!" Energy from her demon powers was rapidly increasing. It was to the point where even the ground was shaking.

"The demon race, power of rage." Madison mumbled, now outside of the ship, deciding not to engage in the situation because of what happened the last time she did that. Instead of her stepping in, two other people did.

"Guess we're just backup for now." Walter stated, cracking his knuckles in preparation. They were now able to go max power, without having to worry about citizens being hurt.

"I think we're all equals at this point." James said.

"The big three against future me. I wonder who's going to win."

BRICK OF SOUND

Chapter 12

STEP UP TO THEIR GAME

"Let's get this bread!" Allie was raised into the air by a crack in the earth, which was an entire block of it. James used his power, element control, to send her flying towards Future Madison. She jumped out of the way, but was frozen in the air by Walter's time control.

"Oh no, I'm being overpowered." Future Madison said, completely lack of enthusiasm. Allie jumped off the floating dirt and used her knee to hit her in the back, right when Walter deactivated his attack.

"You're overestimating your power. Take us seriously!" Walter told her, and she smiled a little. She tossed her cape, which landed on the ground.

"Okay." Future Madison generated a lot of energy, enough to where Ms. Martinez was able to get a good estimate on her full power.

"They won't be able to come close to defeating her if

Allie doesn't accept her true identity. That's great." Allie's demon energy kept on rising gradually, making her lose control of herself at some points. She yelled, charging towards Future Madison, without thinking of it first.

"You're making a bad move!" Walter kicked her before Allie could do anything changing the direction of the fight.

"Out of my way!" After saying this, she gained control of her mind, backing off. Sensing a raising energy behind her, she quickly ducked. Future Madison was hit by a lightning strike from James, amazed by the precision of this attack.

"Dark Flow." She said, releasing calm energy towards the three. They all dodged it, and it went straight past them. But it came flying back at a way faster speed, surprising all of them. Soaring into the group, it went through them and back into the counterpart's hand.

"Guys! Keep your guard up!" Madison called out to them, leaping their way to try and intervene a bit. To her surprise, instead of Mandy, Kandi got in her way, grabbing onto her.

"Don't go jumping in!"

Flashback Begin

"So, your name's Kandi? That's cool." Madison said, trying to bend a piece of metal. Despite the two living in the same room, they never had introduced themselves before. This was the night after Ms. Martinez destroyed Epitomus. "What'd you join for?"

"I really didn't want to become a hero, but because of how my power is, they made me join." She honestly answered.

"Dark flame, right? I could see why they'd make you join. Sub-Legendaries are really powerful, so they're just making sure it didn't fall into the wrong hands. If you don't want them to bother you a lot, I can give you some tips on fighting. I'm no Walter or Allie, but I can still teach some people a lesson!" She proudly exclaimed, getting a small chuckle from Kandi.

"Well, I think you're pretty strong. I was actually really, really impressed with your fight against Alex, and the one with Mandy on Epitomus!" Madison, not used to getting compliments, just shrugged and smirked. She didn't pay attention to the fact that their match was supposed to be private.

"Really impressed, huh? Glad to hear."

Flashback End

"Hey, let go of me! They're in trouble!" Madison yelled, as the attack took its toll. The dark energy, although back in Future Madison, exploded on all three of them, sending them flying all in different directions. Enraged, Madison activated Drive 2 to vanish out of Kandi's grasp and punched her older counterpart.

"You're a waste of my time. I might as well do things my way." Future Madison wasn't fazed. She took hold of her counterpart's arm and threw her back where she came, which sent both her and Kandi flying into the abandoned city. Future Madison vanished disappeared from everyone's sights. A few seconds later, Madison wiped the dust off of herself and stretched a bit, getting up.

"Ugh, that was a hard blow. You okay?" Madison asked, bending down a little to offer her hand to Kandi. She opened her eyes to see the tenor with the sunset behind her, the orange, purples, and yellows blending together.

"Thanks." She accepted the hand, and Madison lifted her up. With the imminent threat out of the picture, there's nothing for them to worry about right now. Except for the fact that their top dogs are gone.

"We've got to go find the other guys. They're our powerhouses, and without them, we can't do anything."

"Why should we? Can't we handle ourselves?" Madison crossed her arms, thinking about what to say.

"Well, yeah, but there's essentially an unestablished power dynamic in the program, just like a food chain. Taking one group out can cause a disruption, and..." Madison went on with her explanation of how the diversity of strength in the band was ideal, and how it works only with everyone in the structure. Unlike Allie or MagnoliaMandy who would interrupt her long talks without another care in the world, Kandi drank in the information.

"Ah, so what you mean is..." Madison never expected someone to also analyze what was going on behind the scenes. Kandi wasn't too fond with heroes before, but after hearing the tenor's ideologies through various practices, it changed her outlook.

"Exactly! It's nice to have a friend who understands what I talk about." She told her, patting her shoulder. Madison thought nothing of the action, but wasn't met with a response. She dropped her smile. "...Right?"

"Madison, I-" Allie climbed onto the island, extremely worn out from how far she was sent, breaking them out of their moment.

"I can't believe I fell for that stupid attack!" She complained, as Madison ran over to her and helped her up.

"How far did you go?"

"I was all the way in Africa! I was chased by a large scorpion!"

"That thing must've been huge! I'll fly you over to the ship." She took her to where the ship was parked, where almost everyone was waiting.

"We got one of them, and now we've got to find the rest." Ms. Martinez said, thinking of possible locations.

"I think they're fine wherever they are. Walter has his motorcycle, and James could just fly up here." Allie told them. As she said that, the motorcycle rose above the island, with the two mentioned on it. They both took off their helmets.

"Or that." Chloe stated, right when they landed on the ground.

"Sorry if we're late for anything." Walter took off his helmet, which he wouldn't necessarily need, but he just had it.

"You're late for us leaving. Let's go!" Mandy responded, landing in front of the entrance.

"Where are you taking us?" Ms. Martinez asked her, with no clue of where her directions are going to take them.

"We can't go anywhere higher than the moon, let alone the land beyond. But there's only one place for us to go." She pointed downwards, possibly hinting at another trip.

"You can call it a back to school trip, while we wait for our first concert. That's of course if our beloved tenor will allow it." Madison nodded.

"Yeah, we've got to catch up with all of our non-band friends. Also with school work."

"Captain's orders. Let's head down to earth!"

BRICK OF SOUND

Chapter 13

LONG AWAITED REUNION

Before Ms. Martinez kicked everyone out for the rest of the day until school ended, they had a small party. It was around 5 am, most people still being asleep. Kendall was in the workshop below the Band House Extended, working on a new piece of technology to be used for someone.

"Then I was about to use Mighty Fist and I got knocked out! That ruined my only possible win ever!" Madison explained, holding up a cup of water.

"Yeah, but you did win." Ash stated.

"No, I didn't! What're you talking about?" Madison told Ash, and a figure next to them slammed a cup of the same on the ground, then shattering it into millions of pieces.

"Dang it. Not again." They said, seemingly either half asleep or drunk. Madison could tell who it is.

"Mary, how did you even get in here?" Ash asked her.

"It's Mrs. Teacher to you! I can go wherever the he-" She fell out of her chair, passing out.

"She's drunk."

"Yeah." Ms. Martinez walked over to the door, about to leave. She turned to face everyone who was up, gaining their attention.

"I've got some meeting to go to, and I have no idea what it's about. I trust you guys can make it to school without me, but Chloe is in charge!" She closed the door, and Madison looked at the Bari in charge.

"Can we go sneak into the band room?"

"No." Madison was disappointed but expected this response from her. She tried to drink her water, but was surprised when it tasted horrible, coughing it up.

"Jeez, the heck's in this?" She complained, taking a closer look at it. The tenor did not remember water being pink and...a little slimy? It was very warming, that's for sure. Madison heard bushes rustling very loudly outside, but didn't think much of it.

"What's wrong?" Ash questioned her. She waved her off, going over to the other side of the room to dump it out.

"It's nothing, it was just a bit stagnant." She began, then turning over to Allie's general direction. "Well, at least Allie isn't in charge. Stop playing Tenor Adventures!" Madison shouted towards her.

"I'm not doing that. You should be training right now!" She responded, which reminded her of how she needed to do that.

"Alright, then I'll pick a new master. Let's see..." Madison looked around at everyone there, until her eyes eventually settled on the one previously passed out.

"How did I get here? Where even am I?" Mary questioned, not knowing of her current location.

"Teach me how to fight, drunk person!" Madison exclaimed.

"You're probably going to die if I fight you." She went back into her drunk form, getting into an unbalanced fighting stance.

"Bring it on, you piece of…" She stumbled, throwing a sluggish punch at Madison. Not expecting much strength from it, she stood there to take it. Since her reflexes didn't kick in, the force from the fist was able to send her flying into the wall, and almost break it.

"Dear god. Good thing we don't have anyone as strong as her in band." Walter said, looking at all of the damage. Mary deactivated it, and crossed her arms.

"I told you you'd die." Madison made her way out of the rubble, hoping Kendall could fix the wall.

"I'm not dead!"

In the future

"Alright, let's see." Future Madison looked around the sky island, deserted like it was in Earthland. Her eyes landed on the moon crystal on the ground. She picked it up, and it began glowing. Coming off of it was an image of a skull.

"What is it?" A dark voice came from the crystal, making the future counterpart of the power user smirk.

"Death, I need a favor."

Back on Earthland

"Since I have no idea how I got here, I'm just going to leave." Mary said, walking out of the door. Madison realized something.

"How are we supposed to go to school without Ms.

Martinez there?" She asked everyone there. The only seemingly rational person was of course Chloe.

"Wait for her to come back, and then we go."

"What if she doesn't come back? When pros get called to a meeting, it's highly likely they won't be back for days."

"That's a great point. I guess we should just chill, maybe do some practice for our upcoming hero exams." Chloe told her. Allie turned off the TV, gaining everyone else's attention.

"There's some real weird energy coming from space. Like, multiple energies. But, they're very far away from us." Madison crossed her arms, smiling.

"Looks like you're accepting who you are."

"I told you already, I'm not the demon princess! Whatever these people are, I'm going to find them. So, if I don't come back in a day, then I'm dead." She flew off through the roof, eventually flying into space.

"She's probably going to die." Walter said, and most of the people that were down there agreed.

"Well, all we have to do is wait." Madison laid down on the floor, as her tenor ominously floated over to her.

"What is it, salad?" She asked it, and the tenor began projecting an image of the meeting. Ms. Martinez had just sat down in her chair, prompting Señora Salcedo to begin speaking.

"We're going to have to go to war with that future enemy. They've obviously got smarts." All of them nodded in agreement, including Mrs. Staller, who was polishing her gun.

"Are we going to have a war like that one against Uni-Corp where we sent one kid and managed to make a peace with them?" Mrs. Staller questioned her, and she shook her head.

"This time we're going to send all we can get. All we

need is permission from the number one hero." Señora Salcedo stated, gaining the attention of Ms. Martinez.

"Yes, you can send my kids into war. Just make sure none of them die, and we're set." Everyone in the Band House Extended that were watching the projection gasped in shock.

"I can't believe she's sending us into a death trap, and me into another." Madison disappointedly said.

"As long as we have the big 3, I think we can win this thing." Chloe told them, trying to lighten the mood. But to her surprise, the members of that group were gone.

"Uh…" They began at the same time.

"What're we supposed to do now?"

BRICK OF SOUND

In Searching through a seemingly endless void of space, Allie couldn't necessarily find the energy, despite being royalty of a demon race. She initially rejected it, and still does, but might come to reason with it at some point. Maybe she will, or she won't. In the end, she's still the demon princess.

"I'm already past Saturn, where the heck could they be?" She questioned, looking around.

"Maybe you should go down." The section leader of the trumpets, Walter, said to her. They had somehow attached oxygen tanks to his motorcycle, and made it all the way to Saturn, in barely a minute.

"Open up a portal to Epitomus. There's a middle section between here and there, and they could be there."

"No." James responded.

"I can't do that, actually. I need a solid surface."

"Then let's use that asteroid over there!" She pointed

over to the floating piece of rock in the distance that was big enough to support the entire band house.

"Fine!" He parked it on the rock, then waited for Allie to fly over there. One she landed herself, he clapped his hands together, which opened up the ground portal. He slammed his hands onto the asteroid, cracking it a little, but ultimately making it large enough to support them. They all jumped in, leading them to the Void. It's the gateway between Epitomus and Earthland, as told by Allie, but since Epitomus doesn't exist, there isn't anything to go to. As the name implies, the void is completely blank, nothing there but rubble from the destroyed Epitomus and the pitch-black darkness.

"So, why are we going into the void again?" Walter asked Allie, who looked at the rocks around them.

"It's the only place we can go without the Land Beyond sending us into court." She answered.

"But how are we going to find energy here?"

"By doing the forbidden, of course." Allie began charging her energy that she was used to.

"Sorry, but I'm not breaking the time laws just so we can find some energy that only you can feel."

"Not that one, the other one." She put her hands together, the same way that Madison did to activate 345, and focused her mind on the demon energy from within her. The rapidly increasing aura came spiraling out, making the other two raise their arms to guard against the overwhelming pressure.

"They're coming from the Future, we have to go to the Moon!" Walter opened up a return portal, and they went through it. With the other two on the trumpet's vehicle, Allie bolted in the direction of the Moon. After landing, she immediately sensed the powers of the ones summoned by Future Madison.

CHAPTER 14: ALLIE'S SPACE ADVENTURE

"This is what you need to do. Infiltrate the heroes' forces and try not to be noticed as imposters. Some of the kids are able to see through illusions, so be extremely careful. I'll take care of the originals." Future Madison told them, and they all nodded at the same time.

"We've got this, master." The fake Ms. Martinez responded. While seeming completely engrossed in evil, she still smiled a little at this, having barely any good left in her. Allie teleported over to where they were, then fired off a large blast at every single one of them.

"I can't believe I have to put up with this, but I can't let them get to earth!" She thought, and the two on the motorcycle arrived on the scene. Before Walter could get off, the gun from the number 4th hero, the fake one, was pointed at his head from behind.

"No interruptions." Him and James put their hands up, not trying to fight. If they did try, they might be hit with a piercing bullet on the off chance, and they didn't want to risk it. Once the smoke from the blast cleared, despite the now big crater, Future Madison was of course gone, but the other three imposters were left.

"The power user isn't here to save you now. That means you have to give it your all or nothing." The fake Ms. Martinez said, and Allie retaliated by charging even more of her seemingly endless demon power supply. But before she could do anything with it, she was quickly restrained by the fake Señora Salcedo. She then escaped, trying to step up her speed.

"Okay, time to be more careful!"

Flashback Begin

"Come on, tell me how strong I am!" Allie exclaimed

to Ms. Martinez, who shrugged.

"If you gave it all you got, maybe you could beat me at half strength. Maybe. Not saying you could, but maybe." She answered. They had just gotten done with DHB practice, and the younger Allie wanted some answers.

"Can you fight me to prove it?"

"No way! You have a lot of improving to do!" This bummed her a bit, as she wanted to fight her.

"How about this? When you're a little older, we can do a sparring match!" Ms. Martinez proudly stated, gaining the interest of the section leader.

"Alright! That's nice!"

"Uh. Okay."

Flashback End

"Let's see what I can do." She thought, then the fake Ms. Stevens sent multiple different kinds of rocks towards her of all different kinds and sizes. Not being able to dodge, she just inhaled the nonexistent oxygen, and let out a big yell. This was able to disrupt the air waves, which generated a portal. The rocks passed through it, and it is unknown where they went.

"Guessing I taught you that. Well, real me." The fake Ms. Stevens responded, having no other explanation of it. Allie simply nodded.

"Hey, we're supposed to be fighting, not making conversations." The fake Ms. Martinez reminded her.

"Oh, yeah! That's right. Well, then why aren't you fighting?" She asked her, which was a great argument on her part.

"Good point!" Walter and James, who were still being held at gunpoint, were amazed by how accurate the copies were.

"That's very weird." The big three all thought at the same time, the other two of course thinking this as if they spoke, they would probably get shot. The sun and moon users rushed at Allie at the same time, who instinctively dodged any damage that could possibly ensue.

"I'm gonna break my back after this is over." She said, then blocking a punch from the fake Ms. Martinez. The two constantly threw punches at her, until the fake Señora Salcedo joined in and kicked her into the air.

"You're not good enough yet!" She shouted, as the fake Ms. Martinez rose up to that level and blasted her into the other two. She came down a bit, charging the biggest blast the group will probably ever see. The fake Mrs. Staller got out of the way, not wanting to be caught up in it.

"See you later, losers!" She shot it at them, and the blast alone was able to push them halfway towards the earth, until eventually dispersing, sending them to the planet like meteors.

"Calling them losers is a little bit mean." The fake Mrs. Stevens told her, and she agreed.

"I should apologize to them later. I feel really sorry."

"It's not like we'll have any time to do that though." The fake Señora Salcedo added on.

"I'll find a way. Somehow."

BRICK OF SOUND

Chapter 15

THE FAILED PLAN

The Big 3 all crash landed right in front of the two band houses, and Madison immediately ran outside.

"What idiots did it this time?" She asked them, skipping the part of asking them if they were okay. Allie crawled out of the crater, on the brink of death.

"That future person made a bunch of hero fakes!" She semi shouted, unable to raise her voice to the height that it usually is.

"We can't exactly get you the best treatment, since Momendez is still gone…" Madison mumbled, seemingly deep in thought about this. The ones that were up came outside.

"I can do it." Mandy responded, breaking Madison's train of thought.

"Great idea, this could prob-" She stopped herself, coming back to her senses completely.

"No way. We still can't trust you after the tournament!" Chloe put her arm on Madison's shoulder, most likely on her side.

"She does have a point. Aside from getting your arm blown off, you haven't exactly done anything for us."

"Stop talking about it and just heal us already!" Allie exclaimed, then almost passing out from it. James and Walter agreed with her, but were heavily damaged from the attack.

"That's what we're deciding! Mandy, just go and do something about them!" Madison angrily stomped off, a bit comically, but still left the scene. Mandy used her power to surround the crater in some form of forcefield, and it slowly began healing them.

"Eventually, a few of us are going to die. We don't know when, but it's really close by." Chloe stated, helping with her with this healing.

"Of course some of us are going to die! You're just stating the obvious!" Allie said, back into shape.

"Looks like someone is back to normal." Meanwhile, Madison was sitting down somewhere nearby the two houses, kicking rocks around.

"I can't trust that many people anymore. They might either turn on me or be some sort of fake." She thought, accidentally sending a rock flying into the sky.

"Looks like someone is mad. What's wrong, 2.0?" Ms. Martinez asked her, walking towards her. Madison got up off the ground and pointed her right hand as a gun at Ms. Martinez.

"Put your hands in the air!" Ms. Martinez did so. Madison began charging a small blast from her fingers.

"What do you have on your wrists?" She questioned.

"Nothing, why do you ask?"

"You're supposed to have the tracker there! You're an imposter!"

CHAPTER 15: THE FAILED PLAN

"Oh. You caught me." Madison dropped her hand, not expecting this as an answer.

"I did that as a joke, but I guess I was right." The fake Ms. Martinez didn't think of it as a joke, but did answer, and blew her cover. She began backing off, not interested in a fight.

"I won't fight you if you keep it a secret though." Madison grabbed her arm, and pointed it right back at her.

"Powernade!" She fired off her now signature attack, which released a lot of smoke, then jumped backwards.

"Or not." The fake Ms. Martinez blew the smoke away, then coughing a little from it.

"Did older me send you?"

"Yeah, she summoned some guy to create me as a copy. I'm supposed to infiltrate your place and pretend to be me, but I don't feel like it."

"Didn't you just beat up Allie and the others?"

"She hit me first!" In front of the band houses, the Big 3 were healed completely by the efforts of the Bari and the Oboe.

"Hey guys, I just got back from the meeting! I'm sending you into war that will probably lead to your inevitable death!" Ms. Martinez exclaimed to them, running towards them.

"That's gre-" Allie began, but then realizing what she said after that.

"What?!" The big three shouted in unison, not knowing of this. Ms. Martinez crossed her arms, not approving of the idea herself.

"Yeah, I don't like the idea either. But sometime after the hero exams, we have to send you guys to fight Future 2.0. Speaking of which, where is she?" She questioned, and it was soon answered by the fake Ms. Martinez flying past her, being kicked by the former mentioned.

"Epic win!" She called out, walking back to their current location. Everyone else was either in shock of the new information, in confusion of what just flew past them, or having no reaction at all.

"What's the issue?" Madison asked Chloe, who was one of the people who weren't completely interested.

"Something about a war, I don't know." She responded.

"Oh. Cool, I guess." Allie grabbed Madison by her shirt, which had skull and crossbones on it, and began shaking her.

"This isn't cool! Some of us are going to die!" She started to get dizzy from this, but didn't care.

"Then don't die, easy." She stumbled on her words, then was dropped by Allie, falling on the ground.

"She has a point." Walter stated. The fake Ms. Martinez rose out of the ground, catching the attention of Ms. Martinez.

"We already took care of Future 2.0. She's being…" Madison looked at her, interested in what they were doing with her.

"…interrogated." At the meeting place, Mrs. Staller had her signature gun pointed at Future Madison's face.

"Tell us everything, right from the start! From when you began your path into that killing spree of yours!" Future Madison was oddly calm, but trying not to be shot dead at the same time.

"Back when I was 12, Chloe is the one who killed all of the civilians. Somehow, she ended up killing Ms. Martinez too, and that triggered 345. So, that thing killed everyone who entered or attempted to leave." She explained. "Whenever I kill someone, for example, that weird person who tried to take 345 out of my body a few months ago, it's not entirely me in control."

CHAPTER 15: THE FAILED PLAN

"Come on, loosen up a bit on the kid. She may have come here to kill us, but that doesn't mean we have to return the favor." Señora Salcedo told Mrs. Staller, who removed the gun from Future Madison's face, still keeping her guard up.

"Do you happen to know what really happened to the past number one hero?" Future Madison nodded.

"I'll tell you, if you try not to kill me. You can keep the chains on me, though." Back in front of the Band Houses, they were finally out of the hole, and James was using his element control to try and fill it in with the surrounding dirt.

"To send you and your friends all back at the same time, we have to find a moon user." Madison mumbled, thinking too hard on an easy to answer question.

"Don't worry, I got this!" Ms. Martinez proudly said, beginning to inhale. Already knowing of the result, Allie covered her ears. The sun user let out a big shout, which made some sort of portal. Ms. Stevens came out of the portal, surprising everyone but her student and hero superior.

"Future 2.0 made a bunch of copy things of us. Can you reverse it?" The latter asked, and Ms. Stevens answered by simply snapping her fingers. All of the copies, in their respective locations, immediately vanished into thin air.

"That was so epic mom!" Madison praised.

"Stop calling all of the pros you meet mom!" Ms. Martinez retaliated.

"I don't call all of them mom. Besides, I've already met my mom before!"

"When?"

"I got lost one day."

"That's very vague." Allie responded.

"Shut it, stupid." Before Madison could access Allie's rage form on accident, Ms. Martinez came to a sudden realization.

"Oh yeah! I was supposed to send you guys to school.

I might as well not do it." Madison looked at her watch. It read 9:00, which sent her into panic mode.

"I probably missed 50 math tests already!" She ran into the Band House Extended.

"Anyway, you guys can go to school tomorrow. I have a day off, since my meeting was cut short." Ms. Martinez began walking towards the bigger house herself.

"I wish I was a part of your hero course!" Ms. Stevens told her.

"I think we should trade places then."

Chapter 16

ORIGIN OF SECTION LEADER

Since Ms. Martinez wasn't available to take them to school, they had yet again another day off. It was good for some of them, but annoying at most for the rest. Madison laid on the middle of the floor, tired from something unclear.

"You need to stop slacking off. At least help us with something!" Allie shouted at her, disrupting her peace.

"Help with what? There's nothing to do!" She countered. Madison did indeed have a point. The only thing that she could help with was on the small occasion they got a special visitor. Speaking of special visitor, the doorbell rang, immediately alarming Mandy into pointing a flame at the door.

"Who goes there?" She questioned, and a mysterious person kicked down the door, surprising the ones of the bottom floor.

"I goes there!" They exclaimed, landing on the

ground. They had a sword, reminding Madison of her mentor in the future.

"And who exactly could you be?" Mandy asked her, dropping the flamed-up hand a bit. They took off their cloak, revealing an older Allie.

"The demon princess, of course! I've came to give you guys information, and nothing more!" Future Allie stated.

"So you are the demon princess." Madison taunted Allie, who crossed her arms.

"Just go ahead and give us whatever information you have for us." She told her future self.

"Suit yourself. I'll just get down to business. Your Epitomus friends are dead, they were killed by Futuexcere Madison. The bodies are either rotting in one of the deserted cities or somewhere in the Land Beyond." Future Allie explained to them.

"Ah. That's...not good I guess." Madison responded, unfortunately not having enough emotion to experience sadness for this moment.

"They were doomed to die a long time ago. Took them long enough." Mandy said, catching her past superior, who was listening in while drinking water, off guard.

"Why would you say that?!" Chloe shouted at her, grabbing Mandy by the collar of her shirt and holding her up.

"It's the truth section leader. Calm down." Madison told her, making the Bari let go.

"I'm going to bed." Chloe began walking upstairs.

"But bro, it's only noon!"

"I said I'm going." She left the 4 downstairs.

"Any other news, princess?" Madison questioned the older Allie, bowing down to her.

"Well, as your future self didn't experience most of the things you went through, she doesn't think of consequences. After making a deal with Death, she made copies of your world's heroes, but since that's too broken, it revived a random person from her time. It could be anyone!" Madison was glad to hear this news.

"That's great! Let's just hope luck is on our side!"

"Wait, wait. You have to explain how you survived Future Idiot's onslaught." Allie said, gaining the attention of Future Allie.

"She almost killed me, but then my demon powers kicked in and teleported me to the moon. She never found me there!"

"Come on Allie, just accept it. You're the demon princess. I will literally bow down for you if you accept it." Madison told Allie. She didn't want to accept it, though. She'll even take that into the grave with her.

"Even though I'd enjoy seeing that, I'm not the demon princess." While the two were talking, Future Allie left the Band House Extended.

"Whatever you say." Meanwhile, in Chloe's room, she was looking at her hero cape, the one that had '#1' on the back.

"I'm sorry…" She mumbled to herself, holding back a few tears.

Flashback Begin

What drives a villain into becoming a villain is kept to themselves for the most part. The only person who knows about Chloe's backstory is the one who took her out of the darkness, Madison. Around 2 years ago, prior to her encounter with Mandy, around the same time Madison met the past number one hero, disaster struck. A mysterious villain had destroyed her home.

"I'm done training, so I might as well go back." Chloe thought, picking up some boxes she used to practice her blasts with, and heading towards the direction of her house. The trees surrounding it were pretty concealing, so it was hard to see anything. But she was able to pick up on the scent of smoke.

"I wonder who burnt something this time." She continued going through the forest, using the smell to guide her to the house. The house was in flames. The boxes soon hit the floor. It was very shocking to her.

"...why don't I have any powers to get rid of flames...?" She quietly said, then dropping to the floor, with tears in her eyes. Her will was strong enough to keep her from completely crying but wasn't enough to stop the wave of emotions. Before she'd have to deal with the sight anymore, a portal appeared below her, transferring her into the dimension of Epitomus. She began falling out of the air.

"Ah! A child!" EP Madison spotted her, catching her before she landed on the ground. Chloe looked up at her, surprised about this entire situation. Her will gave up, and she began crying.

"What's wrong, small one?" EP Madison asked her.

"My home is on fire, and I don't think my family is alive anymore." Chloe managed to get out, as EP Madison was landing on the ground after previously being in the air.

"I can take you in, if that's fine with you. We have some cool people here." She mentioned, letting go of her. Chloe wiped her tears away from her face, now a little happier.

"Okay."

Flashback End

"I'm changing my hero name." Mandy told Madison. Allie had already left to do some mental training under a waterfall.

"Oh yeah? To what? Your villain name?" She asked.

"Something like 'The Inferno'."

"Did your power mutate because of that blast that you shouldn't have taken for me?" Mandy nodded.

"If Fire was mutated, it would become Underworld Flame. If Blaze was mutated, it would become Inferno. So, my power is Inferno now."

"That's hot. Literally." Both of them laughed at Madison's random joke input, then Mandy put her arm around her, and Madison returned the favor.

"How have you been?"

"I'd say fine, but not really. I've been thinking a lot about something." This intrigued Mandy.

"What is it about?" Madison held on to the power amulet around her neck.

"It's time I got rid of this thing and show my full power. After I learned some control over Drive 2, all it's been doing is limiting my potential."

"I got you." Mandy reached behind Madison's neck to attempt at taking off the necklace that was practically stuck to her.

"I don't think you got me." She responded, trying to help her with it. It wasn't coming off though, and it was glowing, strengthening its grip around Madison. It almost began choking her, until it strangely shattered on it's own. Mandy stepped back, so Madison picked up the crystal off the ground. "That's weird. Really weird."

"Yeah…Couldn't tell you why it did that though."

"Oh well, it's what I've been wanting to do anyway. I do feel a new sense of freedom, too."

BRICK OF SOUND

Chapter 17

A SHOCKING DISCOVERY

When Ms. Martinez finished with her meeting, it was now Saturday. Meaning that 8th grade night, which was on a Friday, is less than a week away. Once she walked through the door of the Band House Extended, she called the ones that were present downstairs.

"Good news, we won't be going to war anytime soon. Bad news, we have to do investigating for 3 days, right before 8th grade night. So, you guys will go back to school then." Ms. Martinez explained, dimming the light in Madison's fire of happiness. Yes, her happiness is embodied by a flame. No questions.

"What kind of investigating? Last time we did something like that, a certain someone was kidnapped." Allie asked, looking at Madison, who returned the glance.

"Actually, the last time we did that, you went on a temper tantrum about how you aren't the demon princess."

She countered.

"We're investigating the future. Walter, when I get back from telling the others in the Band House, set up a portal."

"Okay." He responded. Ms. Martinez nodded, and went outside to go talk to the rest of the band.

"Hey, birdman." Mandy began, gaining the attention of Kendall.

"It's Kendall."

"Whatever. You need to make new restraints for the Big 3 guys. Soon, they'll become too powerful." He began working on it.

"How much of a limiter?"

"70%."

"We just got our half strength limiters taken off after having them on for a year! No way!" Allie exclaimed, and Walter agreed. Kendall stopped working on them.

"Madison! What do you think?" Mandy questioned her, then all of them looked at her.

"We need a ping pong table." She answered, completely deadpanned.

"Okay, she's not the right person to ask. I think I know who's the right one." Kendall took out his phone and began calling someone.

"Yo, I'm kinda busy right now. What's up?" Brandon said from the phone, punching iron, until eventually shattering it.

"So, we're in an argument right now. Mandy wants the Big 3 to get heavier weights, but they don't want it. We want you to give the final decision."

"Whatever Mandy says is wrong." He hung up, leaving the group with their answer.

"I'll kill him." Mandy said, clutching her fist.

"How about we do some training before we leave?"

Madison asked Allie. Her response was a swift kick to her face, in which Madison blocked with ease.

"Cool. Looks like you've actually improved from those limiters. But I've improved from the necklace!" Allie continued with a flurry of punches, all at different speeds and strengths. Madison dodged most of them but got hit by some. Her final strike was dodged, that being a good thing cause if she didn't dodge, she probably would've gotten knocked out.

"I've memorized your fighting style against people stronger than you, all you do is move out the way. If you're lucky, you might throw in a blast here or there. You can't land any hits on me if all I do is rush!" Allie taunted, charging at her at a faster rate. Just in time, Madison was able to blast herself out of the way, but Allie appeared behind her to land another hit. On reflexes, Madison clapped her hands together and blasted Allie using her Powernade technique.

"She's not using an ounce of her demon powers. I don't even think Drive 2 could go against that." She thought, then activating the mentioned Drive. Allie wiped away the smoke with a single motion of her hand. Mandy stepped in between the two before the match could continue.

"Either take it outside or take it away. Your choice." She interrupted, as Madison ran out the door, not soon after being followed by Allie.

"Great, now they can't destroy anything in here." Kendall stated. When far enough, Madison clapped her hands together to unlock her part of her 345 form. It was the most she could manage without going berserk.

"Remember, this is sparring. So, don't go all out." Madison told Allie, who made a smug look.

"I'm not even at half of my power, chill." This surprised Madison. The last time they fought, even with the limiters on, Allie was able to beat her.

"Ah, since you're half demon, that means you're technically around 25%."

"I told you, I'm not the demon prin-"

"I didn't say that, but okay." Allie bolted towards Madison, who was able to move more agile. Despite this, Allie was able to keep up with her, with little to no struggle. Noticing how 345 formed mainly on her right side, Allie made sure to attack the left side with harder blows.

"To even be evenly matched with her at such a low percentage, I have to go higher." Madison dropped to the ground and combined 345 with Drive 2 to bring out Drive 3.

"Oh! I thought you said we weren't going to go all out." Allie taunted again. Madison took this opportunity to make a comeback she planned.

"5% of Drive 3 is all I've been able to manage without blowing my body to shreds. So, maybe you're the one who needs to go all out." This comeback would be one of her worst mistakes, though. Allie powered up to half of her strength, until her aura became surrounded by her demon powers.

"I'll give you 10 seconds to say that I win." Allie told her. Madison kept a small smile.

"I'll give you 10 seconds to shut up." She retaliated. Allie appeared in front of Madison and threw a punch, around the same speed as EP Madison's shockwave attacks. Madison caught the punch, but it was so strong that it sent tremors through her arm, almost breaking it. Allie threw another, and the same thing happened again. Madison broke free, then began charging a compressed attack in her hand while upside down.

"Mighty PC Blaster!" The black lightning like short ranged blast sent both of them far from each other. Madison unfortunately got sent flying into rock formation, the force of it making her unconscious. She opened her eyes in what seemed as Power World, but it wasn't. Power World was a much lighter place, but this place was odd, to say the least. The sky was dark, and the only surface was water that was some deep red color, but not of blood.

"There's a weird unbalance in the worlds, so everything is being affected. Don't worry, you're not the only one who will see this." A voice said to Madison, who nodded.

"Any dream you've had of future events is from the original line. For example, the one where you're passed out. That's what was supposed to happen. But, a certain someone, who's gladly out of the picture, changed the course of fate." They continued, and Madison decided to stand up.

"Okay, I understand. So, whoever is behind changing the fate thingy, messed things up for the rest of our world. I'd assume that Epitomus Madison, heck, even Epitmous entirely is involved somehow."

"Yes, of course. That's actually where it started. You see, your mentor was supposed to die back then, but Epitomus did instead. If that wasn't changed, we wouldn't have this conversation."

"You're saying that since our world is already messed up now, I can go ahead and do things that goes against time laws."

"I'm not saying that, but I can see where you're coming from. I'm saying that it's up to you guys to stop Future Madison and put everything back on track. Also, cool coincidence, if you didn't take the power amulet off, Power would've gotten permanently corrupted. Good job on that decision." Madison smiled at this, crossing her arms.

"Of course I can make good decisions. But, before you go, I have one question for you."

"Yes?"

"Can my dreams come true?" The vision that was

given to her began fading away, as she was slowly gaining consciousness.

"I can't directly tell you anything, but I'll just say wait, and something will come to you." Once fully awake, she broke out of the rock, and began walking back to the band house.

"That's going to hurt for a while…" Madison didn't know exactly what direction she was going in, but as long as she could feel the energy, she wouldn't get lost. When she arrived back at the band house, the only person there was Ms. Martinez about to jump into the portal.

"2.0! Don't tell me you got into another fight." Madison avoided eye contact.

"It was a sparring match. Where's everyone else?" She asked her.

"I got a call to just go ahead and leave you guys behind. I think you can manage. But as long as there's no scratches on the tenor, there'll be no consequences."

"Leave it t- ow. Leave it to me!" She responded, trying to give an ok sign but her arms were heavily damaged. Ms. Martinez laughed a little at this, then jumping into the portal. She stumbled into the band house, gradually losing all of the energy she had left. Losing energy made it feel like it was getting hotter, since she feels stronger in colder climates.

"It's hot in here. What time is it?" Madison questioned, walking in further into the room.

"Sometime before nighttime. You've been knocked out in that rock thing for a while." Allie answered, playing Tenor Adventures.

"Honestly, I couldn't even sense your energy coming here. You know how good I am at that. Besides, it's more cold than hot." Chloe also answered.

"I think you're crazy. No way it's cold in here. I feel

like I just got blasted by Mandy."

"Both of us think it's cold, since we lowered the temperature a few hours ago. It's two against one." Allie retaliated. Madison suddenly ran completely out of what kept her running, which made her feel incredibly sick.

"Uh, I don't feel so good." She said, letting out a huge spike of energy. It sent a bunch of gusts of wind around her, going outwards. After this, she passed out cold on the floor, leaving the two there in shock.

"...what?"

BRICK OF SOUND

POWER OUTAGE

Madison had passed out the day before, somehow losing a drastic amount of energy. She woke up in her bed.

"My head hurts." She complained, getting up. Madison was able to keep standing, but still struggling. The 345 markings had stuck to her body, and she was quick to notice. She heard a yell outside, then right after, Allie kicked down her door.

"You're sick! Go back to bed!" She exclaimed at her, as Madison just stared at her.

"Yeah, but I have better recovering speed, now that that necklace is off." Madison stated. Allie materialized a trident like weapon, pointing it at her.

"Sleep time." She put her to sleep using her mind control. Realizing what she did, she immediately got rid of the weapon.

"I'm not the demon princess!" She yelled, leaving the

room. Allie continued walking until she eventually ended up outside. She felt an energy charging at her from behind, so she moved out the way, and saw Chloe flying past her while carrying Madison.

"You're definitely the demon princess!" Chloe shouted, leaving a path of wind behind her.

"Where are you going?" Allie asked her, so she stopped flying for a few seconds.

"It's a meeting that we have. Come out, Kendall!" He flew out the door in his phoenix form, going in the same direction that Chloe was. Madison began waking up, though still half asleep.

"Shut up, Allie. No one cares." She responded, making Allie a little angry.

"One more word out of you and you're dead!" Before she could continue making the princess angry, she fell back to sleep again.

"Time I go. We'll be back soon!" Chloe shot in the direction she was previously going. Eventually, the three ended up in a forest near the Kelli Squad base, as the meeting was held in the forest. While being in the Band House Extended sometimes, Bailey usually just wanders through the forest. No destination, just wandering, searching for something to do. So he didn't burn down the forest, Kendall turned off his phoenix form to then land on the ground next to Chloe.

This part of the forest was amazing. It was a waterfall that went off a very big cliff. Madison thought this would be an even betterer, in her words, a better view at night.

"So cool..." Madison mumbled, now standing. She looked down the waterfall, seeing the water crash down into the river below. This forest was one of the few still preserved in the world, mainly because of its good view. It was created more recently, a few generations after the 3rd power user by some nature power.

CHAPTER 18: POWER OUTAGE

"Shut up, Madison. We need to focus." Bailey told her, making Madison turn away from her.

"We need to focus." Madison mocked, imitating her voice, which made Chloe laugh.

"I'll admit, that was funny, but we do actually need to focus. What's the meeting for?" She asked Bailey.

"The end of the world is coming soon. If word gets out about Allie being the demon princess, who knows what'll happen." She answered.

"I wouldn't say that the world will end but will go into chaos. The government will chase after her until she dies. She'd have to die on farther away planet to not be found." Madison responded, becoming more serious. As much as she could with being half asleep.

"I'm being chased after the government myself. It's not a good feeling. But, it's clearly not a good reason to call us out here. What's the deal?" Madison questioned her, and Bailey clapped her hands.

"Finally, you understand something. The testing for the hero exams is coming up at the end of November, and right after that we have DHB tryouts. The hero exams are an all-out battle royale that turns into a small tournament. For DHB, they only let in 2 tenors and baris. I just hope you're ready for that." Bailey explained, gaining the attention of the duo. Kendall didn't feel the need to get involved with this conversation, so he just sat there.

"I mean, I'll definitely not make it in for DHB. There's so many people bet-" Chloe began, before being cut off by Madison.

"Be positive. You realize that you're the great Section Leader, right? I'm just the low reed nobody without recognition, and even I think I have a chance. It's one of my goals, of course!"

"Then there's the hero exams. There is so many ways

to get points that it's not hard to get the license. Downside is that the Big 3 are competing with us to get their pro license, so using my extremely good luck, maybe I could win over one to my side." Madison continued, getting a laugh from the bass clarinet.

"Your luck is so bad you wouldn't even be able to get a team." Bailey retaliated, even making the usually expressionless tenor smile a bit.

"Your luck is so bad that you couldn't even make 1st chair." Madison countered. Bailey almost blasted her in the face, but was blocked by Chloe, who negated the attack.

"Alright guys, chill. One of us just has to train and train until they're able to handle a lot of strong warriors all on their own, and the other has to deal with the other." Chloe interjected. Madison got extremely heavy weights put on her arms, and Bailey was teleported into the band house.

"These are even heavier than that gravity...!" Madison fell down to the ground almost instantly. Due to already having some form of sickness, she coughed up blood.

"Once you're able to stand, I'll put you into the gravity machine. You'll be able to catch up with your age." Chloe told her, vanishing into thin air. After this day, Madison trained until Ms. Martinez came back. 8th grade night went by fast, they did a performance for a day, so they decided the day before the hero test that they'd fight each other to prepare each other.

"Bring it on, tenor!" Kim exclaimed, throwing a smoke bomb at Madison. She jumped out of the way, and was constantly bombarded with more and more grenades, blasting all of them. She was eventually high up into the air, so Kelli sent up multiple water bullets towards her. A thunder cloud appeared above her, striking the ground with lightning, after being missed by Madison dodging.

"You guys really don't know how to fight an idiot!"

Allie shouted, flying up to Madison.

"Oh, so the demon princess wants a piece of this?" She countered, charging a blast. She fired it, only for it to be deflected with no issue. Allie constantly let out small compressed blasts at her at a rapid pace, trying to get her to drop her guard. When Madison visualized something cracking, she ducked below Allie and blasted her with her 'Powerful Blaster' technique.

Madison dropped down to the floor, laughing at something she thought of.

"Guys, you can stop trying to kill me now. Let's take a break." She got up, then walked towards the Band House Extended, before stopped by Mandy, who grabbed her arm.

"Come with me to the waterfall."

BRICK OF SOUND

Chapter 19

ORIGIN OF THE INFERNO

They went through the forests, as Madison was confused as to why she was even being led out this far. It didn't necessarily make sense to her, but she still followed along, due to being intrigued.

"You've brought me all the way here, what gives?" Madison questioned, but was caught by the beautiful scenery. Sure, the night sky was black, though the moon reflected off the water. In her opinion, the waterfall made it better. Mandy was staring off into the distance but looked back at Madison.

"It's nice, isn't it?" She asked, and Madison nodded. Nice wasn't the full definition to it, as it was really nice.

"I mean yeah, but that doesn't answer my question." She responded. Mandy let out a sigh.

"I brought you out here as I want you to know something before I go." Madison's eyes widened a little bit.

"Before you…?"

Flashback Begin

Mandy was born to a family of trained assassins on sky island. Humans on sky island had evolved over generations to have the ability to fly at birth, as they have wings. Unfortunately for her, she didn't earn this. Sky island humans look down on humans, figuratively and literally. Since she didn't have the ability, the downside is that her race, including her family, didn't accept her. To the point where when she turned 8, she was kicked off the island.

Two years later, she lived alone in the wilderness. Of course, the closest place to where she lived was the waterfall. The view was just fantastic in her eyes.

"What's this?" Mandy thought to herself, as a portal opened up below her. Before she knew it, she was falling into the dimension of Epitomus. She activated her telekinesis to stop her from hitting the ground too hard.

Some years after this, she was eventually found by Chloe, and they went on to make their villain organization. Despite seeming to be chill, her race is of hardened killers of humans, which means she was occasionally ruthless, but generally didn't care. That's until she came in contact with the heroes.

When she met Ms. Martinez, her evil side was more at bay. Mandy had learned how to control it since she didn't want anyone finding out about her affiliation with sky island. The sky island was eventually destroyed by EP Allie, but she didn't care.

To deal with her sadness, her competitive side was created by Brandon. She'd argue with him practically every day, and with them sitting next to each other, it go to both of their benefits. Their arguing helped the both of them.

"You call yourself a Bari? Your playing is trash!" Mandy shouted at Brandon, during practice. This was sometime before the Band Festival started.

"I don't here you practicing, so you can't talk! This Bari is beat up, not my fault!" Brandon retaliated.

"At this rate, you're just an 'Oversized Alto'!" During the time Chloe was gone and Madison was held captive, Mandy had to lead the band. Eventually, she came in contact with the one who destroyed her home island.

"I've destroyed your home island. How does that feel?" EP Allie asked Mandy, as they were in a clash of fists. Even though she was a little surprised, it wasn't enough.

"Oh, that was you? I thought it was someone more important." Mandy countered. She kicked upwards, sending EP Allie flying up into the air. She teleported above her and punched her in the back, going down quickly into the ground. Right when she came in contact with it, she fired off a large amount of her blaze energy.

The smoke dispersed, revealing Mandy holding EP Allie's arms behind her back, so she couldn't use any blasts on her.

"You want to become number one, right?" EP Allie questioned her.

"One more question out of you and you're dead." She answered. EP Allie laughed at this response, not taking it seriously.

"Wouldn't it be bad if you had to bear the same fate as your race?" She continued asking questions, but before Mandy could let out a blast strong enough to get rid of the ongoing problem, she appeared behind her. EP Allie blasted Mandy with her stolen power, it being so large that it would be able to take out a building.

Mandy wasn't obviously defeated by the attack, but it left a scar on her back. A big one was there, where her wings should've been. The scar was there to bring back the horrible memories of her childhood. EP Allie vanished, leaving her there.

"I don't need another scar." She said, then getting up off the floor. Even while being heavily damaged, she still thought it was a good idea to walk all the way back to the Band House. Halfway there, Brandon eventually found her.

"You're a bad fighter, just charging in like that." He told her, and Mandy put her hand on his shoulder.

"Shut up, idiot." She began falling forwards, so Brandon caught her, not wanting her to injure herself anymore.

"You're the stupid one."

Flashback End

"That's what you need to know. Aside from the fight with the stupid villain, I haven't told anyone about this." Mandy finished explaining, now looking back off into the distance.

"So, you're sky human. That scar on your back, no one's seen it before aside from Brandon." Madison understood now. Mandy began walking forward, a little too close to the edge of the water.

"Yeah. I would show you it, but now it's time I go." She turned back around to face the tenor.

"What do you mean by go?" Madison asked her, as Mandy began falling backwards. Right when she saw this, she started running towards her and reached out her hand. She was too late though, she was off the cliff before she could grab her hand.

"**A**re you serious? That idiot..." Madison thought to herself, then jumping off the waterfall. When crashing into the water, she immediately locked her arms around Mandy. Using some sort of power, a shield surrounded the two of them, blocking out all of the water.

"Why would you do that?" Mandy asked her, as Madison removed her arms from her.

"Ah, I thought I could've died! Forget what I just said. It was impulse." She freaked out for a second, then gaining her senses.

"Answer the question." Mandy demanded.

"Fine, if you want to be annoying. You just jumped into the river with no context, so I had to get you out of there. If you died, the timeline would've been a big disaster." Madison answered.

"You've been suspicious since you betrayed us that

time ago. What's your deal?" Madison asked her.

"I want to prove to you that you're the best." Taking her by surprise, the shield disappeared. Her body acted as a life jacket, lifting her out of the water. Mandy took her out of the water.

"I'm no way the best. You've seen that yourself. Those Big 3 guys are on an entirely different level!" Madison spat out water. For some reason, Drive 2 activated, and she instinctively jumped out of the way to evade an oncoming blast from the oboe. Very well aware of her weakness, Mandy used Tenor Turbo to dash below Madison in order to get to where she would land before her. Madison prepared to fire a blast at point blank range but was met with a punch to the gut, unfortunately still above ground level.

Though phasing in and out of consciousness, she managed to gain it on time to kick Mandy in the face, but fell on the ground.

"Weakling. If you don't want to end up like me, expect the unexpected." Mandy told her, as Madison was still catching her breath.

"I won't be wasting any time! Get up if you don't want to die!" Mandy exclaimed, using her Alpha Black Fire technique to provoke Madison into dodging. She of course did get out of the way, but that punch did do a lot of damage.

"Who're you calling weakling?" She choked out, charging towards Mandy. Copying a tactic from Allie, she constantly fired blasts at her, all of them being countered.

"You're the one calling yourself the weakling. You've underestimated yourself so badly you can't even fight with us anymore!" Mandy absorbed a blast from Madison and used it to appear behind her and was quickly found out.

"I can't even think of a strategy!" Madison called out, activating Drive 2 to kick her away from her.

"Who needs a strategy when you finally have a chance

for a real battle? I'm giving you a chance to win." Mandy said to her. This didn't reach to her, just made her angrier.

"I've never won. It's all circumstance. No matter what you say, my wins are always losses!" Madison noticed that Mandy wasn't even going all out. Neither was she, but that was because she didn't want to hurt her. Mandy wasn't going all out just to taunt her, at least in Madison's view.

"Bring it out." Mandy told her.

"...what?" Madison asked comically, despite the situation.

"Your dragon moves! You're supposed to be one step ahead of me, but now I'm stronger! How does that feel, loner? Going back to square one, I suppose?" She taunted, this managing to get through.

"Shut up." Madison responded, the Drive 2 turning into Drive 3. The lightning was red instead of black.

"Maybe I'll just take your throne of Low Reed King. You're more like the king of losers." Reaching the breaking point, the lightning dispersed. She began walking towards her, which soon turned into running.

"They aren't losers!" She blasted herself into the air to avoid another hard hit, which at that point could've killed her. Drive 3 had basically fused into her base, but she didn't notice.

"You're the leader of them, so who am I not to expect all of them to be bad?" Mandy asked her, launching herself in the air. Madison breathed in some air.

"Dragon's Power: Roar of Destruction!" She let out the burst of air, the energy being of the color of Drive 3's new color. It still had the flame effect to it, so Mandy easily blocked it. She dropped her guard after it was gone.

"You still haven't passed me." She thought, bolting towards Madison who was now on the ground. Having leveled her feet to gain the upper hand, she dodged the attack.

Due to her clumsiness, she soon ended up on the ground.

"A fight at this hour?" Ms. Martinez questioned, viewing the explosions from afar. Madison made her way up before Mandy could.

"You challenged me to a fight, and you can't even beat me. Maybe I'm the cool one." She stated, kicking into Drive 2. The blue steam had become a darker shade, signifying that she had gotten to a new level.

"Scorching Heat!" The aura came out as a burst, even catching Madison by surprise. The power up was new, therefore inexperienced. Having had dealt with this before, Madison knew of the inevitable time limit.

"Oh, you really want to go all out? Your loss!" In Madison's language, someone going full power is all just a challenge for her. She can't stand people not taking her seriously, and this was her chance for someone to finally see how strong she had gotten. For the first time in a while.

Madison dashed towards Mandy, only to be put on the defensive once she got close. Mandy was trying her hardest just to get her to stop blocking so they could get this over with on time, but she didn't budge.

"Every time a small opening comes, she just counters with a punch as hard as she can. This battle isn't weakening her, it's making her stronger." Mandy got hit by an uppercut from Madison, sending her flying into the air, and she followed her into it. Madison grabbed her by the face, shooting back towards the ground at a greater speed, then firing a large blast.

"Surrender." Madison stated, having the past villain pinned to the ground. Even though she planned on turning the tables, she would be stopped by their teacher who just arrived.

"Who hit first?" She asked surprisingly calm.

"It was me." Mandy told her, making the number

one hero sigh.

"Alright then. You're not going to be able to go to the hero exams, and Madison will if she can pass the test." Ms. Martinez gave them the consequences. Madison coughed up blood from the punch from beforehand.

"Okay. Just take us back to the Band House." She said, getting up off the floor. Mandy followed suite, behind the shadow of the number one hero. Ms. Martinez began walking back, so they followed.

"You're not half bad." Mandy brought up to Madison, breaking the silence. As this was one of her mini goals come true, she smiled a lot more than normal. This small goal was to impress one of the ones above her, so it just fueled her ambition even more.

"Of course I'm not bad! I'm going to be number one!" She claimed, being hit on the head by Mandy.

"No, I am!" Instead of going into their usual bickering, they just laughed instead. Once they arrived at the Band House Extended, Mandy went straight inside.

"I'm proud, kid! Not for breaking the rules, but for your determination." Ms. Martinez gave her a high five.

"Me, determination? Not believable." She laughed off the compliment, walking into the door. Right when she closed the door behind her, she was met with a kick over to the opposite side of the room.

"Why did you do that, idiot?" Allie landed on the ground, being the culprit of the attack. Madison got up, dusting off her pants.

"What did I do...?" She questioned both her and herself.

"You survived!"

BRICK OF SOUND

Chapter 21

HERO EXAM PREPARATIONS

For the hero exams, they get grouped up with a pro hero and prove that their worthy of joining the hero ranks. Madison has to do a small test against Ms. Martinez before she can go.

"It's been a few months since we last sparred, mom! But this time, it's so I can be a part of the exam thingies." Madison said, clapping her hands to make a spark of her shockwaves.

"Just remember that the guys who made it in last time had to do the same thing, so don't drop dead on me." Ms. Martinez responded, gradually increasing her power.

"No promises, but I might be able to. Show me your challenge!" She boldly exclaimed, and the aura rapidly came out of Ms. Martinez, putting similar gravity pressure like Future Madison's down onto the tenor. She tried activating Drive 2 to be able to get around quickly, but that wasn't even able to help her move at all. Her aura got larger and larger, until eventually making the shape of the sun itself, obviously not as big.

"T-this is too much…for me to handle…" Not even her thoughts she could say out. The crushing pressure almost brought her down, but she focused her energy on standing.

"How's that pride you just had doing?" Ms. Martinez asked her, and Madison looked up to smile at her.

"Give me more." Immediately after she finished the sentence, the pressure from her sheer energy alone sent Madison down to the ground. She was completely unable to stand anymore and couldn't move at all.

"Do you admit defeat yet?"

"Yes. I do." Madison finally gave up on trying to stand up to her teacher, who cut off the overwhelming aura from getting any bigger.

"How do you feel now?" Ms. Martinez didn't give off the steam because of the modified Tenor Detector she had on, which kept her power steady.

"No one has ever followed behind me in my footsteps, and I want that to happen. I want people to acknowledge me." Madison began.

"That's why I've got to become number one, so people will realize how cool I am. I've always loved and looked up to people, but no one has ever returned that to me…" Tears started to form in her eyes, even if she didn't want to cry.

"But I can't become number one because of me being chased around by the villains. All of my friends are in danger by just being by my side."

"All of them are leaving me behind, and it's really bothering me. I can't do anything to help it, though." A single tear fell from one of her eyes. She looked back up to Ms. Martinez.

"What do I do?!" She thought about this for a second, and finally came up with her answer.

"If you're going to be my future successor, then show the entire world what it means to come from a background of no success!"

"I've never lost to anyone, since I've always wanted to protect everyone. But you can be the different story, someone who's won and lost their battles, and when they've lost, came back stronger than ever!" Madison got up from the floor and wiped the tears out of her eyes.

"There's never been anyone truly by my side. I can't keep this up for long." Ms. Martinez put her hand on her head, which stopped Madison from rambling.

"Then I'll be by your side until I eventually die." Two hours after this, they finally got to the place to prepare. Not a lot of people wanted to prepare, but this would get them an extra chance to boost their score on the hero trials. No one has seen the scores except for the heroes themselves, so the kids would be able to see them after the preparation.

Due to how powerful they are as a unit, the Big 3 were separated into different teams. They got to pick their teams, and it was usually edited by Ms. Martinez to the point where the teams were actually compatible to a point. Instead of all fighting at once like in the actual exam, the others had to stay and watch the fights unfold.

"Come on, guys! Start fighting!" Ms. Martinez exclaimed from the crowd.

"You were supposed to start it!" Madison shouted back.

"Oh, yeah. You guys can begin!" Ms. Martinez allowed them to fight. Madison, Chloe, and Allie were facing off against Señora Salcedo, the number two. Before any of them could blink, the latter kicked all of them in the face, then appeared back at her original spot. Madison held onto where she was hit.

"Ow, so fast!" She said, charging towards her teacher.

Each attack was gracefully dodged.

"Woah, so cool!" The number one and number three hero both said at the same time, despite working together most of the time. Chloe took out the Universal Sword and fired a slash of energy towards Señora Salcedo as a distraction, but it didn't work. Due to her battle experience, she's very adept at focusing. Chloe then followed after Madison into throwing attacks left and right at the hero.

"No one has ever landed a successful hit on her in her time as a professional. It's honestly amazing." Madison thought, as Allie vanished behind Señora Salcedo, trying to hit her with the trident. She just simply moved out of the way, and Madison lifted her arms to block the weapon.

"You can't even use it properly! Aren't you supposed to be a pro?" Madison taunted. Allie quickly got rid of the royal weapon and went straight to trying to land a hit. Ms. Martinez started eating popcorn, enjoying this match. Allie, mad that she couldn't land a hit, brought her rage form. The demon's strong strength comes from the anger they have from within. It's the source of why she's usually screaming all of the time. With her royal bloodline, it gives her a higher power bank to draw out of.

"Out of my way!" Allie bolted towards Señora Salcedo, who was surprised at the sudden burst of speed. She didn't falter though, as she still dodged the attacks. To her disadvantage, Allie just got more and more angry after every miss, meaning she got stronger gradually.

"Then there's the hard hit!" Ms. Stevens shouted, as the 2nd best hero knocked Allie out of both the rage and consciousness with a single kick. Señora Salcedo looked at the two that were still awake.

"You should be more careful." She said to the duo, luckily for them they could understand her.

"Madison, use that blast thing!" Chloe exclaimed

to the tenor, who understood what she meant. Madison clapped her hands together, beginning to generate a small concentrated blast in between her close hands. It got brighter and brighter over time, so the Bari decided to use this chance to stall. Before she could strike with the weapon, it was shattered by Señora Salcedo. This surprised the cold-blooded villain turned good.

"Oh no! My sword is gone! Wait, I could just make another." She realized, materializing a slightly bigger sword. Madison fired off the blast at Chloe, who jumped out of the way. Right when the hero dodged, the shiny attack exploded, being extremely bright. The only person not affected by the blinding light was Madison and Ms. Martinez, the latter who was basically the sun herself. Though, she just so happened to have on sunglasses. Madison thought she was just cool like that.

"Tenor Turbo: 2nd Turn!" Madison used a move like her Powercut technique, which was essentially an uppercut on her teacher. After that, she followed her into the air to use Power Hammer, but was interrupted by Allie moving in between the two and firing a blast that was extremely powerful.

"Look who's awake." Madison told her, waiting for the outcome of this attack. After the smoke dispersed, it revealed Señora Salcedo holding up a white flag, which meant surrender. She wasn't damaged at all, though.

"Alright, alright. I lose."

"Good job, Madison!" Kim shouted at her from the crowd, earning a thumbs up from the tenor.

"That was definitely all me!" She responded.

"Hurry and get out of the arena, it's my turn." Bailey said to Madison, jumping out of her seat and landing on the ground, soon being followed by James. Madison gave Bailey her signature thumbs up.

"I hope you fail."

"You probably didn't even pass." Bailey countered. When the number two hero returned to her seat, Ms. Martinez did an overdramatic jump onto the semi arena.

"Alright, both of you or who goes first?" She asked, stretching a bit. Bailey stepped forward.

"I'll go!" Using her light powers, she teleported at the speed of light in the direction of the hero. Her kick was blocked by Ms. Martinez, who blasted her after doing so.

"Come on, make the light scythe!" Ms. Martinez excitedly thought. Of course, the bass clarinet did it, filling the pro with excitement. Before she could fangirl about it, lightning bolted towards her fast, but she dodged it. Now in the air, she was faced by Bailey and had James on the side behind her, not being a good idea. Some rocks rose out of the ground, the larger ones, and were thrown at Ms. Martinez. Being aware of her surroundings, all she had to do was move her head around and the stones flew past her. Completely switching tactics, Bailey rushed in, throwing the scythe at her. It missed, but it was grabbed by the clarinet section leader and thrown at Ms. Martinez. She caught it; the force of the catch strong enough to shatter it.
"Oh, darn it! It's gone!" She complained, then regaining her composure. Lightning bolted towards her again, this time being blocked and deflected by the hero. It was dissipated before either of them could take damage.

"If you want us to go full power, then you should take us more seriously." James told her, as Bailey agreed. She let out a burst of energy, signifying she had stopped holding back as much.

"Okay. If you say so."

Chapter 22

ALL OR NOTHING

Ms. Martinez charged energy in her fist. She attempted to use the energy fist on Bailey but missed by a hair. She tried to return with a punch herself, but also missed.

"Hey, is it okay if I actually go all out? Would I destroy anything?" The hero asked through blocking attacks from different sides.

"Go all out, I'll fix whatever is broken! But that doesn't mean you can intentionally break things!" Ms. Stevens shouted back as an answer. After gaining a response, she returned both of their attacks with full scale blasts. Bailey dashed through the smoke, almost landing a blast of light on Ms. Martinez. But it was successfully evaded by her propelling herself upwards. Due to her energy being mostly heat, her aura was also progressively getting hotter.

"Is it getting hot in here, or is it just me?" Madison questioned.

"We aren't inside, and if we were, it's not just you." Allie responded.

"You ruined the joke!" Rock after rock flew passed Ms. Martinez, the arena had essentially turned into a light show. Bailey had been using light attacks so bright she eventually had to stop. Ms. Martinez had to stop raising the heat or she would've burned everything.

"So, we're around equal footing now, with you two fighting me. Neat!" Ms. Martinez said.

"I've seen enough. I forfeit." Ms. Martinez told them, gliding back to her seat.

"Aw, come on! We couldn't even see anything! Why give up now?" Madison asked her.

"For the reason you said. What's a good fight if you can't see anything?" Madison nodded after receiving the response, as it was a good point.

"Hey, mom! Is it ok for you and mom to take me to get ice cream if I pass the hero trials?" She then asked Ms. Stevens.

"Of course we will. Isn't that right, 'The Martinez'?" Ms. Martinez crossed her arms.

"Yeah, yeah, whatever. You have a practice round too, don't you?"

"Oh yeah! I almost forgot. I'll see you when it's over!" Realizing it was her turn, she jumped to the arena floor.

"It's your fight too, idiots! Go to the middle thingy!" Madison shouted to Ash and Kim, neither of them were paying attention. They did go to the arena, not wanting to be blasted by her.

"You don't have to tell me." Walter said, slowly floating over to the stage. Around this time, you'd say something like, 'It's been 3 books, why haven't we learned what Ash's power is?' Well, your question is going to be soon answered.

"Finally, a chance to shine." Kim stated, pulling out a

smoke grenade.

"Nope, my turn." Ash interrupted, as a dark cloud shadowed over the unnecessarily large arena. I mean, it's the one for the hero exam. So, not unnecessarily large for that, but unnecessarily large for this.

"What's the weather broadcast for today?" Madison yelled out to her from the crowd.

"Oh god." Walter said, wanting to get the fight over with already.

"Cloudy with a chance of l-" She began, before being kicked out of the way by Ms. Stevens.

"Maybe if you didn't waste any time, your team would've stayed at 3. But, until she wakes up, hopefully," She told them.

"You'll have to team up." Kim threw down the smoke bomb, yet it didn't go off. Walter had frozen it in time.

"We'd need 3 to even stand a chance. We forfeit."

"So early. Oh well. When do you guys want to see the results?"

"Show us the money!" Madison yelled, hopping down into the arena. She picked up Ash off of the floor. In advance, the highest scores will have a certain amount of points on their head at the start of the exams. The largest amount you can have is a million and the lowest amount (that's passing) is 500. If you don't want to be targeted as much, you would hope to make around 1000 points.

After the ranking spots were given, some of the people there went to the next challenge. To fight the strongest person on Earth.

"Alright! So, you kids want to fight me?" Mary questioned the group of 6.

"You're the same age as the rest of us!" Madison responded, crossing her arms. Mary put some limiters on her wrists.

"Okay. Let's fight."

Chapter 23

THE WORLD'S STRONGEST

"I'll be the one showing you guys the battle royale part!" Mary exclaimed to the group of 6.

"Oh, really? You can't take on all of us at once." Bailey told her with confidence. Mary simply smirked.

"I'd like to see you try." James lifted both Allie and Madison off the ground and shot them towards Mary using air, but they were both effortlessly dodged. Walter appeared behind her and tried to get a good hit by using the distraction. With speed and force not even the one with control over time could handle, he was knocked out with one punch.

Chloe charged in with the energy sword. The all-powerful weapon was stopped in its path by one finger.

"What?" She questioned, before being swiftly punched by the unstoppable force. Right when the bari hit the ground, Bailey and James went in. Bailey got close to blinding Mary, but she was kicked away into a rock. Mary tried kicking James, who managed to block in time.

"A worthy contestant?" She unleashed a flurry of punches at the clarinet, that were all dodged. Once he attempted at a counter attack, Mary immediately decked him. The attack sent him flying.

"Power Strike!" Madison came in from above, almost landing a hit, but it was dodged.

"Jeez, I'm not even drunk yet, and I've already taken out 4 of you guys. Really says a lot about that band of yours."

"You're just absurdly strong! Shut up!" Madison responded. She's right though. The Big 3 was taken out successfully in little to no time by one person.

"Forgot about me?" Allie asked, teleporting next to Mary. She hadn't dropped her guard, so she used a sledgehammer like attack to slam her into the ground.

"I don't want to fight you, so let's just wait for Ms. Martinez." She told the tenor, who nodded. The number one hero appeared, seemingly on command to being mentioned.

"Looks like you have a new record! 45 seconds!"

"Well, I haven't been slacking off on my training. See, I have a new training buddy here." She grabbed and picked up Madison.

"One that's severely outclassed. Oh, I forgot to ask. When's everyone waking up?" Madison questioned Mary.

"Give them a few hours, they should be up. I don't think I killed them. I think." The day went by smoothly after that, and the auditions did too. All they had to do was wait for the hero exams. Unfortunately for them, Future Madison broke out. She was very angry. She had found out about her family lineage, in her timeline respectively. She's the child of the head family of the One's Above.

A quick history lesson. There were a few families that claimed to be related to those in the 'Land Beyond' that rose to power in Earthland. The Earthlanders were quick to believe lies like those back then, and still aren't skeptical about it now. Of course, people like Future Madison didn't believe them, even while young. Where they reside is an underwater city, which is the city of gold.

You may ask, why's Future Madison mad about this? It's because she's born to oppose them. At least, that's what she thought. They're held in high regard, if they ever were to show up on land, you're supposed to respect them. But, there's always people born to rebel. Future Madison now has more hatred for them, due to initially not knowing of her family. 19 years of solitude, now to find out her origins?

Once she broke the bars with ease, she bolted out of the now open window, making her way towards the Band House Extended. Allie was chilling on the roof of the building with Ms. Martinez.

"Why do you think my parents left me here?" She asked Ms. Martinez, who shook her head.

"They didn't leave you here. They sent you here because they knew Epitomus Allie was going to destroy the planet."

"Do you think they wanted me?"

"Of course they did. It's just they knew they wouldn't live to see another day after they sent you. Think of the bright side, you have a family now. I didn't take you in for no reason."

"...You're right. Thanks, Mo-" Madison fell down from the sky and landed on the roof. Ms. Martinez got up.

"Woah, what's the problem, kid?" She had a bit of a coughing fit, but then regained her composure

"Future me is on her way here, and I don't know what she wants!" Being able to sense energy from a far distance, Ms. Martinez dashed in the direction of Future Madison. They stopped in their tracks and faced each other.

"What is it?" Ms. Martinez questioned the escaped

prisoner.

"Where's the city of gold?" Future Madison asked as an answer.

"Go look in the oceans. I know you'll find it." She answered. Somehow able to release all of her anger at once, she disappeared in the eyes of Madison and Allie. But Ms. Martinez was able to see her go.

"Kids, we have to go underwater."

"A fishing trip? What's this band come to?" Madison mumbled, as Ms. Martinez landed back on the roof.

"We're going to the city of gold, idiot! Just make sure you know the difference between normal people and the One's Above." Allie countered.

"Oh, that place! I don't think you should tell me to know the difference. I'd tell Mandy or Chloe!" Madison pointed out.

"Good point. Both of them would be a big problem. Either way, pack your bags. We'll get on the spaceship tomorrow." Ms. Martinez, told the two, making her way down the building.

"Another trip? This'll go on borders with Carowinds." Chloe stated, listening in from the living room.

"Not surprised you were eavesdropping." Bailey retaliated, not having the same enhanced hearing powers as her. Madison and Allie followed Ms. Martinez into the building.

"I assume Chloe has heard everything. So, I task her in getting the flute travelers back here by tomorrow. Kendall, you go get the rest of the low reeds and the rest of the Kelli Squad." Ms. Martinez tasked the Bari and the bassoon. Kendall wasn't in the room, but she knew he was listening from the workshop.

"Where are we going exactly?" Kim asked, not supposed to be there but was anyway.

"If you want the specifics, we're going to Single

Town." Madison laughed.

"Wait. That place really exists?"

"Yeah, what's the issue?"

"Nothing." Kendall walked out of the stairway and made his way to the door. Chloe followed him out.

"Hey, mom. Aren't we supposed to like, you know, go back to school?" Madison questioned the hero.

"Until this issue and another is solved, we can't go back. Maybe we'll be back by January."

"Alright then. Band trip to Single Town!"

BRICK OF SOUND

Chapter 24

DEEP IN THE DEPTHS

After gathering everyone together, they made their way to the ocean in the revamped ship. It had to be adjusted to the ocean, so Ms. Martinez told Kendall to upgrade it. While in the water, Madison focused on looking out the window. She was mesmerized by the view. Most of them were glad of this, mainly cause Madison never shuts up when put in a conversation.

"Looks like someone's excited." Allie taunted Madison, who was smiling. Of course, it broke the smile.

"Shut it. You should be excited yourself. You know, it's the city of gol-" Madison retaliated, before being hit in the face with a rock.

"Jeez, just being honest! You always beg for my tournament money!"

"One more word out of you and you're in the water!" The Power user crossed her arms, not wanting to argue anymore. She looked back to the window.

"Fine."

"So, who's stronger down here this time?" Mandy asked Chloe, reminding her of the time on the way to Caelum Insula.

"Whoever's noble blood, I think. I'm assuming Walter's going to be that one." Chloe answered, gaining the attention of the trumpet.

"Nope. I've already done my research; I'm not related to them." This conversation got the tenor interested too.

"Maybe we can find out about my family too. Never met them before, and I don't even know if they exist or not."

"Looks like we have something else in common." Allie told her.

"How about it, Alex? What've you flutes found so far through your adventures?" Chloe questioned Alex.

"Aside from being followed around by Mary sometimes, nothing interesting. Knowing her, she's probably at the city of gold right now."

"True. Oh, looks like we're getting close!" Madison exclaimed.

"There's a lot of water down here." Allie stated.

"...we are literally in the ocean." She responded, then getting up to go get some of the others. She walked into the room where Kim was.

"Get up. We're almost here."

"Give me 5 more minutes." She said bluntly.

"You aren't even asleep! Come on!" Eventually, they came in contact with the bubble around the city. There were multiple parts to this land, and they landed on the beach side of it. There were no people there, so it was the perfect place. Ms. Martinez walked out first, scanning the area.

"Alright guys. Keep in mind, most of you guys might be wanted here. They view upcoming heroes different than me. So, I'd advise t-" Ms. Martinez began, before seeing

Mandy casually strolling past her.

"I'm heading into town to get some food. Anyone want to go?" Madison walked out the door and sat down next to the ship.

"You can handle yourself. Just don't cause trouble." She told the oboe, who continued on her way. Before she could fall asleep, Allie stepped in front of her.

"Where do you think they keep the gold?" She asked the tenor. Madison opened one of her eyes.

"Even if I did know, I wouldn't tell you. Taking gold from this place is like taking an ancient artifact from its museum. Unless you want to lose your heroes license, I wouldn't try it."

"Why do you guys feel the need to talk about committing crimes when I'm right here?" Ms. Martinez questioned Allie.

"Oh yeah! I need to go to Single Town." Leaving the question unanswered, she left the two outside to go on some quest.

"Huh. Weird." Ms. Martinez thought. Meanwhile, Mandy had made it into one of the towns somehow unnoticed. While she was walking, one of the One's Above had entered the town. All of the people there had gotten out of the path of them, all but Mandy of course.

"Hey. Watch it, kid." They said to her. Since they didn't have bodyguards, without hesitation, Mandy immediately went to blast them. But she was stopped by being quickly knocked out of the way and into an alleyway.

"You idiot! Why would you do that?" A voice asked her. Before Mandy could answer, they covered her mouth and escaped to some form of safe place. It was an underground base, though not very lively. The only person there was Mary, who was drinking some water, presumably from the water next to the beach.

"Back already? That was quick." Mary said to the person, motioning to them to sit down, and they complied.

"You're saying that as if I don't do that often." They countered.

"Wait a minute, Mary. Who is this person?" Mandy questioned Mary.

"Guess I forgot to introduce her. This is Rayven. Come on, sit down with us." Mandy did so. Mary took out a notepad.

"Alright, so how much trouble did our little client here cause?"

"Not much, aside from almost killing one of those above idiots." She wrote that down.

"Oh, looks like we have another rebel! You'll definitely fit in here. We have another person tagging along with us, but they aren't here right now."

"I can't stay here for long, I told everyone I'd bring some food back." Mandy brought up.

"It's fine, I'll stop by there soon. What brings you guys here to the city of gold?" Mary asked her.

"Future Madison is supposed to reign terror here. I personally don't care about this place, but I hate her. Anyway, why are you guys here?"

"You know me, I'm just a traveler. Rayven escaped from those above guys after ending up here a few years ago and came across me. We've been chilling down here for some time. Here's your reward." Mary tossed a gold coin at Rayven, who caught it.

"Is this a chocolate coin?"

"No, no! It's real this time. The gold down here may be common place to you, but it's extremely rare there."

"Even if I haven't been up there in years, I still don't trust you. But I'll give you the benefit of the doubt." A figure emerged from the stairs.

"Back from spying on those idiots." A voice all too familiar to Mandy said, catching her attention immediately. It was her rival, Brandon.

"It's you! Why are you here?" Mandy and Brandon both shouted at the same time, pointing at each other. Currently at the ship, Madison was supposed to be keeping guard outside, but ultimately fell asleep. She felt a spike of energy nearby, so she got up, alarmed by it. Madison got into her fighting position, looking around.

"Alright, what is it now?" Madison asked, as the area around her went pitch black.

"Go underground. Go to Single Town and look underground." A voice told her, similar to the one she heard months beforehand. Madison sighed, then dropping her guard.

"You could've just told me when I was awake. But, guess I have to go anyway." She woke up and began walking off. She was stopped by Chloe.

"Where do you think you're going?"

"Single Town, you know, that place we specifically had to go to. Yeah, that place." Madison poorly explained.

"I'll keep guard. You probably have some business to attend to, not that I know of, but something." Chloe responded, standing in Madison's previous place. Madison gave her a thumbs up and ran off, trying to navigate her way through an area she's never been in before. Before she knew it, Madison, being Madison, ended up in front of a coffee shop.

"'Coffee for One?' My kind of place." She walked in, and the place was relatively empty.

"Finally, a customer for toda-" Allie started, rising from behind the counter.

"What are you doing in Single Town? Shouldn't you be in the other town?"

"I'm here cause I own this place. It's my coffee shop in this deserted town. What brings you here anyway?"

"A voice told me to look underground, so I thought this was a good spot." Madison told her. Allie lifted up a trap door that lead to something below it.

"I knew this was here for something. After you." They walked down through the entrance. Whatever was down there was surely technologically advanced, more than anything else in the city of gold. Despite being advanced, it seemed to be outdated.

"Hey, so if you wanted one thing to happen, what would it be? It could be anything!" Allie tried to fill in the silence. Listening to their footsteps only got a bit aggravating. Maybe just for her.

"Anything? Well, I'd wish to live with my family. I probably don't have one, but if I did, that would be great." Madison honestly answered. "If I woke up and had a family, I don't know what I'd do. But I'd definitely be happy, since I never grew up with one like everyone else."

"Aww, how sweet. I hope that dream of yours comes true." The tenor couldn't tell if she was mocking or being genuine, so she just waved her off.

"What's the government up to this time…?" Madison mumbled as they reached a dead end.

"Do you want me to blow it up?" Allie asked her.

"No, I have an idea." Madison placed a hand on the wall, and it activated a scanner. It accepted, so it opened up. She stared into the area, very confused.

"I didn't think that would work." They continued into it, until finding a table with notes on it. Allie picked them up, realizing it was in a different language. It was in demon, so she could understand it.

"This paper is around 100 years old. It's saying something about a project." Madison now could also understand demon for some unknown reason, so she nodded.

"Project Xenos? That kind of rings a bell. I'm pretty sure Xenos was the one who created all of the powers about 10,000 years ago. Then they disappeared 100 years ago." Madison remembered.

"Yeah, and no one knows where they went. I think the Ones Above have something to do with this."

"So, what are we supposed to do? No one's gonna believe some kids shouting about some project." Allie got an idea, so she began dragging Madison back up the stairs.

"Then we've got to get followers!"

BRICK OF SOUND

Chapter 25

PROTECT THE PRESIDENT

"Alright guys, we've got to make a plan! We're in a government protected place, so too many heavy hitters, and we're gonna get chased. Meaning Amy is out of the question." Alex started planning out on the table, surrounded by the majority of the people present.

"I can control my explosions." Amy retaliated.

"Yeah, but they won't do enough damage." Alex countered.

"Future Madison is going to be hard to beat. Then we're going to need everyone we can get." Chloe said from outside.

"She's right. Either all of you guys and me defend the place all at once, or we can get some backup. By backup, I mean the best we could ever get." Ms. Martinez told them, reading through some mission assignments.

"What kind of backup?" Bailey asked her, the question then being answered by Mandy teleporting back into the room.

"Back from shopping." She stated.

"What took you so long? And where's the food?" Bailey questioned her. Mary appeared, carrying both Rayven and Brandon in her hands.

"I'm here." Mary responded.

"...bad jokes aside we still need something to eat. I would send Kendall out, but he'd attract too much attention." Ms. Martinez began thinking.

"What do you mean by that?" Kendall asked comically. Mary dropped the two in hand.

"She's got that. Just give her a few seconds." She pointed over to Rayven, who vanished. Of course, after a few seconds, she re appeared with a ton of food.

"I stole from about 4 stores. Where's my change?" Rayven asked Mary.

"I'll give it to you later, we have business to discuss. Brandon, since you know them better than the rest of us, try to convince them that we won't try to backstab them."

"I personally don't trust you after you knocked me out in one shot." Bailey countered.

"You can just ask Madison. I won't try anything as long as she's on your side. She's my training buddy. By the way, where is she? I haven't seen her around anywhere." Chloe walked in, disregarding her guarding position.

"She had something to do in Single Town. No clue what it is, but she probably has everything in control."

"Hey, are you guys underground heroes?" Amy asked the trio, which earned her a slap on the wrist from Ms. Menendez.

"That system should not be mentioned down here! Not even normal citizens know about that!"

"...Underground heroes? There's another group?"

Brayden inquired, cracking his knuckles. There were surface level heroes, the ones known around, such as The Menendez. But, there's now another system?

"Yup. We met a few of them when we were travelling as the Flute Travelers. They're pretty formidable, some way stronger than us. They're masters of instrument combat, like Flute Style." Amy explained to them. "Flute Style is quick and effective movement, trying to get rid of the opponent as fast as possible. There's tons of potential for that."

"Not even hero experts know about this system, where 'Underground' comes from. That's the reason why you never heard about the number zero hero." Ms. Menendez added on. "Before the position was opened again, he was the head of the organization. He was the operator of all investigations, secret missions, and anything with secrecy."

"So, to answer your question, no. We really do work on our own." Mary told them.

...

While this discussion was going on, Madison had on a completely different change of clothes. She was wearing a black tuxedo and had on a golden crown. Madison was standing on a building, which had a large crowd in front of it.

"Your president needs your assistance, my people! A copycat version of me will arrive here in some time and will destroy us all unless you can help me and my army! Will you fight with me?" Madison exclaimed to the crowd. They surprisingly all cheered, which put a smile on her face.

"It's almost as if she was made to do this. They practically worship her, as if she was their savior." Allie thought, sitting down next to her.

"President! What should we do if we're powerless?" A voice shouted to Madison from the crowd. She pointed her fist towards the sky.

"Then get your weapons and do your best! Arm yourselves, get into position, then prepare to fight your hardest!" Madison told them. They cheered again, making her smile again.

"Finally another one of my goals completed. I just need a few more." She wrote her thoughts in 'Orange Juice Recipes'.

"President, shall you save this town, we will give you all of the riches you desire!" Another voice said to her.

"Aw, come on people! Keep your gold to yourself, I'm not into that stuff." Madison responded, then thinking about it.

"On second thought, I accept your proposal. My people, I must go to my resting place. We shall start the revolution when I return!" Madison, along with Allie, went back to the spaceship.

"Oh, look who's showed up! It's the president!" Mary attempted to tackle Madison, but she quickly moved out of the way.

"No way! Woah, am I actually the president? Wait, why are you guys looking at me weird?" Madison asked them. Aside from the obvious ones, everyone was confused as to why she was wearing the outfit.

"Before you ask, she's the president of Single Town. The entire town fell in love with her instantly." Allie explained.

"That makes sense." Mandy and Brandon agreed at the same time, despite not wanting to.

"You're saying that we have an entire army on our side? Even better for us. Just remember not to kill her, we need to keep her captured. I'm looking at you, oboe." Ms. Martinez said.

"Either way, you should've gotten something more

valuable than the trust of them. What else did you bring?" Mandy asked Madison. She took out the notes on Project Xenos.

"This! It has connections to the person who made powers. None of you guys will be able to read it though, since it's in demon. Allie's still reading it."

"Okay then. Are we going to get ready to fight, or what?" Chloe questioned everyone.

"Of course we are. We've got to eat first, right?" Mandy responded.

"Oh, wait. I just remembered. I have a new idea. Training buddy, I'll need your help for it." Mary told to the tenor.

"Sure, I'm up for it. What's the plan?"

BRICK OF SOUND

Chapter 26

Z CLASS MISSION

Future Madison had calmed a bit after she broke out. She had been looking around all of the oceans, and finally found the city of gold. Able to breath underwater, she began generating a concentrated blast in both of her hands. Her plan was to wipe out the entire thing in one go. Mary appeared in front of Future Madison, which confused her.

"Hey, you look nice. What do you say to a drink sometime?" She told Future Madison, who laughed.

"You see, I'd love to. But I have a job to do."

"Then what about a quick fight?" Future Madison stopped charging the blast.

"Sure. Sounds interesting." Mary threw a punch at her, so Future Madison blocked it. But, it sent her flying backwards. Future Madison dashed back to launch an attack herself. Mary kicked her in the face, stopping her from going any further.

"My power is Drunken Fist. What's yours?" Future Madison backed up a bit.

"I'm still unsure, really. All I know is that the one I received was taken away from me, but then I found out I had another."

"It was that blast, right? Can you show me some of it?"

"Since you asked so nicely." Her aura came out, slowly getting stronger. Mary tried punching her again, and Future Madison countered with a blast. She dodged by going upwards. Down from the top of the spaceship, Madison had changed into her hero outfit, and was watching the fight from binoculars.

"Looks like it's going smoothly. Kim, go command the town." Madison commanded her, so she gave a salute.

"At your wish, president." Kim jumped off of the ship to make her way to Single Town.

"When should I go in?" Ms. Martinez asked, as Madison was over the planning. Normally, it would be a horrible idea, but she studied it heavily overnight.

"Once Future Madison agrees to go to the surface. We'll put the ship on another level to follow her there and try to capture her."

"That plan isn't half bad."

"You came up with it yourself." Mary dodged all of the blasts Future Madison tried to land, pretty successfully too. Almost like she knows every move she makes.

"How about we take it to the shore? You know, the one the sun touches." Future Madison then remembered her previous plan.

"But I have a thing I need to do, I can't d-"

"Let's make a deal. Forget whatever you were doing so we can fight without anything holding us back." It surprisingly convinced her easily.

"Alright, sure." They vanished, which alerted Madison, still watching but from a window on the inside.

"Guys let's go! Kick into maximum overdrive!" After her command, the ship began rising off the ground. There were engines built in the bottom that were activated, shooting them upwards. When the two appeared on land, waiting for them there was the Big 3 themselves.

"Oh, hello. Fancy meeting you here." Allie stated.

"Wait, how much will we get from this?" Walter whispered to her.

"Mom said that if we're lucky, we'll get ranked up to professionals. That's how Z Class Missions work. It's either a rank up or a big reward." Allie whispered back, disregarding Future Madison still there.

"So, are we going to fight or not?" She asked Mary, who answered by activating her power.

"I'm not leaving without one. Now, come over here you…" Future Madison used the advantage to dash towards her, only to be swiftly dodged and hit with an uppercut. Since they were going all out, Future Madison did cough up blood but managed to stand back up again.

"Time I busted out the big guns." Future Madison said, revealing her mechanical arm. The same blast she used against Brandon was being charged, the cursing energy sending chills down their spines. Before she could fire it, the spaceship launched out of the water. Right before it landed on the ground, Ms. Martinez jumped out of it and punched Future Madison hard enough to where she was knocked out of the attack. Everyone else aboard the ship got out.

"You're my favorite hero, you know that? Strong and ready to fight at any time. I wish I was like that." Future Madison claimed, clapping her hands together. The gravitational force came out instantly, then bringing everyone down. Mary was unaffected, but she was passed out somewhere nearby, so she couldn't help.

"You've forgot about someone." Madison joked, then laughing. She walked over to Future Madison and stared up to her.

"Don't you know what a trap is? You still haven't learned your lesson from the festival!" Mandy shouted out to her.

"Do you think I care if it's a trap? I won't die." An evil aura gradually surrounded her, not being 345. Future Madison tapped her, similar to the move she used back in the Hero Trials, but it didn't work. Madison smirked.

"Isn't it nice to get out every once in a while? It's like I haven't seen daylight in years." Future Madison blasted her with her metal arm. When the smoke dispersed, Madison wasn't unaffected. The aura was acting like a shield, yet she wasn't acting like herself.

"I'd advise going along with what she says, kid. Negative Drive is a force to be reckoned with." Ms. Martinez told Future Madison.

"Why should I trust you, you might be blu-" Before she could continue, Madison used her hand alone as a cutting attack, and it severely wounded Future Madison.

"I'm pretty sure the hero said for me to not kill you. I really want to, but I can't bring myself to go against orders." Madison said, putting chains around her future counterpart. After the chains were on, the gravity was lifted off everyone. Ms. Martinez got up to pick Future Madison up off of the floor.

"Good job, whatever you are. Can you bring our tenor back?" The aura died down, once completely gone, Madison sighed, not knowing where she was. Did she sleep-walk...?

"How'd I end up here? I thought I was in the room thing."

"Room thing? What's that?"

"It was called the Room of Mind and Truth or something. Mary took me there, and now I'm here."

Flashback Begin

"What's this place?" Madison asked, looking at the metal door. There seems to be a lot of things underground.

"It's a room that brings out your most unused emotion, of course. The room will simulate what your mind looks like. Go ahead, walk inside." Mary explained, opening the door. The exact moment Madison stepped foot in the room it turned into the place she sees in her dreams sometimes. The endless body of water. She looked around.

"I don't feel anything. Besides, I don't have emotions that much. What could be the most unused?" Madison stated.

"Oh, just wait. You're going to feel something." Mary told her, then closing the door. The door behind her disappeared, leaving Madison trapped in the area.

"Most unused, huh. I'm the tenor, I can handle whatever it is." She mumbled. Tears started to build up in her eyes, so she quickly wiped them away. They kept coming, though.

"Looks like our confident, uh,' tenor', was it? Never mind. But, looks like you've came to confront me for the first time ever." Madison with the evil aura appeared behind her.

"Leave me alone, Negative Drive!" Madison quickly turned around to face the drive, who shrugged.

"I mean, I'm here cause you're more vulnerable now. More power to me, since I can control you. You're nothing more than a mere vessel." Negative Drive said. Madison couldn't stop crying, so she just closed her eyes.

"I'm not going to let you control me."

"Or what, you're going to be useless like you always are? That's how you ended up back in the Hero Trials, remember? You couldn't do anything back then, and you can't do anything no-" Madison punched Negative Drive, but it didn't even phase her. "My point proved. Just remember, I'll always get stronger. I might even be able to break out. I won't hurt those heroes you're friends with. Before I was put into you, I had to make a vow not to when I'm in control."

"Just leave already! Your voice is super annoying." Madison shouted. Negative Drive slowly vanished away. When she was finally gone, she felt an excruciating pain in her body that made her collapse on her knees and cough up blood, which seeped into the water.

"I knew I was weak. Besides, why me anyway? I don't deserve to have Power, but I can't give it away. I'm stuck with these problems, and I want to get out of them. For them to just leave me alone once and for all." Madison began.

"I don't think it's my fault, but I'm pretty sure it is." She was going to continue, but the door appeared again. Mary opened it, causing Madison to get off of the floor.

"You ready to head back?" Madison wiped away her tears.

"You know it!" Right as she got up, Mary disappeared from her vision, and she felt a warm presence behind her. She turned around, facing a person. They were around her height, wearing a black cloak that covered their entire body. They took their hood off, revealing long, wavy hair.

"You're so close to the truth. We'll be waiting for you." Madison stood there in awe. The person, she never met them in her life...but they looked so familiar. Like she'd known them her entire life.

"The truth?"

"Let's just say there's more than what you think out

there."

"Hey, what's the hold up? There isn't anything there." Mary spoke up, gaining her attention. When she looked back at the person, they had vanished. Madison simply shrugged, just assuming it was Negative Drive playing mind games with her or something.

"Sorry. I thought I saw a fly…a really big one."

Chapter 27

WHAT'S SINGLE TOWN ABOUT?

Now that she was the president of Single Town, Madison had a job. To take care of her people, of course. She could make new friends, maybe learn new things, and add more valuable gold to her collection. Madison loved collecting things, especially small things that she finds in unknown areas. But, she also collects figures of Ms. Martinez, her favorite hero.

"This one is the one from the hero trials! Isn't it cool?" Madison asked Chloe, who nodded.

"Yeah! It is!" This time, the gold would be of higher value. Gold doesn't exist normally on Earth, so the main source of it comes from the city of gold. Luckily for Madison, the One's Above don't like messing with Single Town, it having the lowest population. They don't know the amount of gold they have, though.

"I'm heading out mom!" Madison exclaimed, putting her backpack over her shoulder.

"Just remember to bring me back a souvenir!" Ms. Martinez responded, so she ran out the door. The ocean was far away from there, but she'd be able to make it in under an hour. Maybe at a faster time if she accidentally ran into Mary. Usually when she takes on missions, she has her get her to the destination faster, most of the time at a price.

"That'll be 10 dollars." Mary stated, opting for Madison to pay her.

"What? Come on, I'm the president! I have to make sure my people are safe!" Madison exclaimed.

"10."

"I'll just give you this gold coin, so I won't have to pay you for a while." She handed her the coin, so Mary picked her up.

"Don't do anything stupid." Mary threw her in the direction of the city of gold, which was across the state. Not even a minute later, Madison could already see the ocean below her.

"I could've just taken saxophone salad." She realized, crossing her arms. Eventually, she did start slowing down. But, she abruptly stopped in the air, and looked down.

"...oh no." Madison plummeted out of the sky and down to the water. Once she hit the water, her speed got a little slower, but she still went down extremely fast. So fast, that when she landed in her office, her body wasn't wet at all. Allie was waiting in her office and was surprised by the loud crashing noise from behind the desk.

"Yo." Madison said coolly, rising the desk with finger guns. Allie wasn't affected in the slightest.

"No."

"Dang it. Wish it worked."

"Maybe in an alternate universe where you're the luck

jackpot. It exists somewhere."

"Good point. I don't care why you're in my office right now, so I'm just gonna go." Madison got up and put on her crown. She jumped out of the hole now in the roof of her office and landed gracefully in the middle of the street.

"How's it going, president?" Kim asked her from afar, running towards her. Madison shrugged, then opening one of her eyes.

"Not a lot, just waiting until January. Trying to meet more people to boost my chances." Kim showed her a paper, seemingly a mission assignment.

"I have just the thing for you, then! C-Class, get the people underground to move into Single Town. Not that anyone wants to come here, but it's better than an abandoned empty gold mine." Madison took the paper and ran off, not knowing exactly where she was going, but it was a good start. Her first stop was to look in the secret hideout that Mary showed her, so she kicked down the trap door.

"What's up, losers?" Madison walked down the stairs, only to find Mary alongside 3 people she's never met before.

"Who're you calling loser? You look like more of a loser than all of us." One of them replied.

"Shut up, Junior. You're talking to the president." Mary responded.

"There's a president?" One of them asked, then being punched by another.

"Yes Wix, there's a president! Even I knew that!" They shouted.

"Alright then, president. What's your business with us?" Junior questioned Madison, who was looking at a nugget of gold in her hand.

"Just wondering if you'll join us in Single Town. We have a ton of jobs open." Mary began pushing Wix closer to the stairs.

"He's immortal, and we don't need him. He can join."

"No way! If I'm joining, then you're all coming with me!"

"Wait. What're your powers, then? I already know Mary's, so…"

"I can make lotion." Junior said.

"Very practical." Madison said sarcastically.

"I can't die unless someone kills me." Wix stated.

"Guess you're going to stay in Single Town for a while."

"I can summon the dead and make them a part of my army." The last one said.

"Ah, useful." Madison responded, no one knowing if she was joking or not.

"Yeah, Alayna has the only somewhat useful power out of all of us." Mary sat back down in her chair.

"But you're literally the strongest person on Earth!" Madison countered.

"I don't have control over my power most of the time. It's either completely random or I start it myself."

"Kind of like Mrs. Staller's gun?"

"Yes, like her gun. Anyway, sure. We'll join your town." Madison smiled a little.

"Great. I have business to attend to, so I'll see you guys later!" She ran back outside and clapped once. In a few seconds, saxophone salad appeared in front of her.
"Ready to go full speed?" The tenor glowed green from within the case, so she got on it and it began floating. Without warning, it shot out of the bubble, then eventually the water, so fast that she wasn't drenched from it. Meanwhile, from the Band House Extended, Chloe and Mandy were watching the sky from the roof.

"A shooting star, nice." Chloe said. Mandy squinted a bit.

CHAPTER 27: WHAT'S SINGLE TOWN ABOUT?

"Doesn't it look like it's getting closer?" Chloe looked at her with a look that said, 'Are you stupid?'.

"No, obviously not. Well, it does sound like it's screaming." Chloe changed her focus back to the bright light that was coming in very fast. Before they could identify who it was, Madison simultaneously crashed into the both of them at once. The tenor landed gracefully, however.

"We're famous now, by the way." Mandy told Madison while lifting her off of her.

"Why?" Madison asked, steam coming out of her again.

"We protected the city of gold. So, basically, our band is popular around the world now. People would die to watch our events in person." Chloe told her, dusting off her pants.

"We'd sell out in less than a second. I've got to reward you guys after this." Ms. Martinez said, then landing on the roof herself.

"Does that mean I can get ice cream?" Madison questioned her, very excitedly.

"Yes, we can get ice cream. But first, we've got to do midterms. You guys can meet me at the arena tomorrow morning."

"Wait a minute. How can we do an entire midterm arc when there's only 3 chapters left?"

"Simple. Jump cuts."

The Next Day

"Alright, here are the basics. The more popular section leaders fight the heroes, and if they win, everyone in the section passes. Of course, there's the written test, but who really cares about that. It's fun to just fight, right?" Ms. Martinez explained.

"What about me?" Mandy asked, since she was the only oboe.

"You get an immediate pass." Ms. Stevens answered, and Ms. Martinez agreed.

"What? No fair, mom!" Madison exclaimed, putting her crown on the empty seat next to her.

"It's okay. We'll get ice cream after this. First, let's have the first battle. Try not to d- I mean, try to win!" Ms. Martinez shouted.

"Let's see here…uh…oh, right! The flute and clarinet section leaders shall fight against the number 4 hero!" Suddenly, the arena was moved to a different island, which was somewhat tropical.

"Not to plan, but we'll roll with it." Ms. Stevens said, and Ms. Martinez nodded.

"I can't really use my gun in midterm tests, so I could just pass you guys." Mrs. Staller told the two.

"Okay." James responded.

"Guess we're moving onto the next fight, then. Stevens, it's your turn." A large explosion was heard near the arena. Ms. Martinez immediately got up and blasted off to the direction of it.

"Of course there's an interruption! There's one every time!" Madison complained, following her by running. Chloe summoned her sword to then toss it at Madison, who fumbled around with it before catching it.

"You want to take a try with it?" Chloe asked the tenor. She swung it around a bit but then almost fell over, since she was running.

"Sure. I'm probably gonna be the last one without a weapon, so it's nice to have one."

Chapter 28

LEGENDARY CRYSTALS PRINCESS

Madison doesn't have a sense of direction, something she somehow got from Ms. Martinez. Every time Chloe went one way, she went the opposite way.

"We've got to go right." Chloe reminded her, as Madison crossed her arms.

"Nope. It was left!" Madison countered. Chloe pointed at the smoke coming from the right.

"If you want to go left, then go." Madison sighed, then following the Bari into the forest. Meanwhile, two of the Big 3 had already gotten there.

"Looks like some people have stumbled upon my land. Welcome to my grand domain!" A voice stated, neither of them knowing where it came from.

"What's your play?" Allie questioned them.

"Your power is mind control, right? I've got half of that. I'm pretty sure you can do the math."

"It's the mind. I don't want to deal with this, so I'll just take my lea-" Walter attempted to walk away but was stopped by an invisible barrier.

"Let's see what the state of your minds combined looks like." They snapped, and the area around them turned into a wasteland. Similar to Madison's, but not completely water. It was basically completely sand.

"Oh god. Not the scorpions!" Allie exclaimed, getting flashbacks to when she got blasted to Africa.

"Relax. There's clearly no scorpions. Pretty sure we're in some sort of pocket dimension or something." Walter told her. They heard an audible crashing noise.

"Alright, I've dug through memories to find some things." The voice stated, turning on a screen in front of the two.

"What's the point of this, anyway? You're clearly not going to kill us." Allie asked.

"So quick to assume things. A magician doesn't reveal their secrets."

"You're clearly not a magician." Walter stated.

"I've got some stuff from the past, and even the future. What're you the most interested in?"

"Tell me about the end of the demons." Allie said.

"Suit yourself."

Flashback Begin

What really happened to the planet of the demons? This is what happened. EP Allie, somehow her age was seemingly the same, had blown it up. Right under her nose, though, flew a small ship through space. The ship was Allie's.

They had to send her to earth, or else the demons would've found out about her existence.

Her existence alone goes against the laws of both the humans and the demons respectively.

Somehow, she managed to survive completely alone and soon blended in with the humans. Fortunately, she was found by Ms. Martinez, who gave her her name. The now number one hero took her in and lived with her until the band house was built, making her some form of mother figure.

"Try doing this!" Ms. Martinez shouted, firing a blast. Allie copied her movements, making a blast herself.

"Woah, that's cool! I've never done that before." She did it over and over, before stopped by the number one hero.

"That's what it's like to be my daughter. It's like I'm seeing myself in my younger days." Ms. Martinez stated proudly.

"But you're not that old." Allie reminded her.

"I know! But still." She wasn't too early to awaken her demon powers, nor too late. But, demons get stronger as the rage builds up in their bodies, right? Her being half demon counts that, but also counts her improving through training.

Since the Big 3 were limited to strictly half of their power, that meant they couldn't go above or below it. They were stuck to improving their base for a long time. Sure, it was efficient, but some of the people they fought before and lost to won't be coming back for a while. So they can't get any rematches from them.

Allie initially met Madison during the 5-month period of the destruction of the UVC and the building of the original Band House. Despite their connections to the number one hero, neither of them had even came in contact with the other prior to this.

"When can I move?" Madison whined, covered in

bandages. Before then, her body was burned severely after her fight in the tournament. Those scars would stick with her forever.

"In December we can let you out, but you'll still be in bandages from head to toe." Ms. Martinez told her while in a chair next to her.

"Dang it. I'm really hungry." Madison mumbled. Allie walked into the room and dropped her bags next to the door.

"I've got the missions completed. And who's the mummy?" She asked.

"Look, I have no clue who you are, since I can't see. But you sound stupid." Madison responded.

"Okay, okay. Don't respond, Allie. I don't want Madison to break any more bones than she already has." Ms. Martinez calmed down the situation.

"I'm interested in finding out what you look like. Who knows, you might be a prince or something." Allie said to Madison, leaving her mission stuff on the ground and beginning to leave.

"That's really creepy, but I can say the same to you too. I bet you look worse than you sound." She countered.

"Likewise." Allie grinned, then walking out the door.

"...I can't counter that cause she's gone."

Flashback End

"Here's the deal. You can either stick here for a few weeks, or one of you can take a lot of pain." The voice gave them a choice. Walter and Allie looked at each other.

"I'm taking the pain!" Allie shouted.

"No, I am!" Walter shouted back. This continued until they decided to do rock paper scissors to decide. Walter chose paper while Allie chose rock.

"You win this time. But, if we ever get in this situation again, I'm taking the honors."

"I know." During this time, Madison ultimately ended up getting lost. She knew about this place; it was called the Deep Forest.

Two people are selected to learn something from the past or future, and once that's out of the way, they have to make a choice. Either way, it always ends up with a battle that leads with the villain on top. The villain was an anonymous illusion master that knows what people are afraid of and their deepest secrets, including memories. They're good at predicting the future, with theories of them having the power to see it too.

With Madison's case, they tried continuously to get her over to their side. Madison denied it all of those times, without hesitating once.

"I'll give you more information on your past family's death." They tried. Madison kept the same expression.

"No." She pondered what they just said. Family…? "Wait, I had a family?" She asked to herself, not wanting them to find a weak spot. As far as she could remember, family was one of the things she didn't have. All that came to her mind was whoever her mentor was…

"Then what is it that you desire? Money? Power? Fame?" The voice interrogated her.

"Find out yourself, then." At this point, Madison had her arms crossed with the sword floating next to her. Sure, they couldn't find any desires, and there weren't many things in the past that interested her.

"I can tell you about your fate." Madison blinked.

"Not joining your side, but I'm sure you can do that for me. We're one alike, right?" She asked, hearing the voice laugh a bit.

"Yes, we are. Telling you completely would go against the rules, so I'll tell you partly. It involves a letter." Madison nodded.

"Ah, yes. Letters. A great thing. Alright, what do you want me to do in turn?" Madison put her arms back to rest.

"Are you fine with ending your journey?" Not thinking twice, the tenor placed her hand on her stomach.

"Sure, if that's what it costs!" Before she could blast herself, the other hand grabbed the other. Negative Drive had gained control for a moment, so Madison is trying to break free.

"I just became President of Single Town! We can't do this!" Negative Drive went back to doing it.

"Yeah, it's not me, kid. That weird person is controlling us!" They would've continued arguing, but they were ultimately stopped by them blasting themselves.

"Good bye, Power." Madison fell to her knees. Since she blasted her stomach, of course there will be repercussions. She threw up a lot of blood. A lot. There was now hole in her body. Madison smirked before falling backwards.

"Nice."

Chapter 29

EVERYONE'S GIVING THEIR ALL

As her sword regenerated, Chloe clashed with the copy of her best friend, Madison.

"Look, I don't want to fight her. Just leave me alone!" Chloe told the voice, who laughed maniacally.

"You're the Bari, right? You're supposed to overcome your fears. What happened to that villain side?" The voice mocked. Wanting to prove herself as the Bari, she sliced through the illusion of the tenor straight down the middle, which turned her into a leaf.

"Does that satisfy you?" Chloe countered, as the sword disappeared. The voice just laughed.

"So, you're willing to end even your best friends' life to realize your dream?" The Bari grinned, the evil side still being there.

"She'd be fine with it, so sure. I'm not just going to give up on something I've already done." It began raining. Allie and Walter had been let out the desert, the latter taking the risk. When they appeared back on the island, they were separated from each other. The trumpet barely managed to get up off the ground.

"If I get to the arena soon, maybe I won't die." The battle damage was high, but he was durable to keep himself alive for a few minutes. That's what he did. Walter managed to make it to the front of the arena without dropping dead, since that's what he was going to do then. He fell forwards but was caught by someone.

"We have to fight together." Allie said, as Walter looked at her while barely alive.

"What am I supposed to do? Just die?" Walter responded, as a blast came flying towards them, coming in contact with something and exploding. The culprit was Ms. Martinez.

The blast was completely blocked by the awakening of Walter's weapon, a shield. The outcome of course ending with him passing out, the protection fading.

"Oh, you guys are real! I'm sorry, I thought it was another illusion." Ms. Martinez ran over to them.

"Illusion? Where exactly are we?" Allie asked her.

"You know that S Class Mission that's always been on the list? We're there. I'm pretty sure you can heal Walter on your own, because I need to check on Madison. Knowing her, she's probably lost." The demon princess nodded.

"Yeah, you're fine. Just make sure she isn't dead." Ms. Martinez began running, doing her best in attempting to not get lost. She did stumble upon Madison not soon after.

"That's not a good start for the tenor." Ms. Martinez picked up her body and teleported her back to the arena. Chloe made it back to the arena around the same time as her.

"Section Leader…" She stumbled, then trying to use her healing powers on her. It was working but had a slower effect than usual.

"How do we stop the villain?" Mandy asked Mrs. Staller, as they were on a different part of the island.

"Easy. See something suspicious…" Mrs. Staller pointed a gun at a tree that was oddly out of place.

"…Shoot it." She shot it with one of the piercing rounds, so it went straight through the tree. The voice behind everything appeared, now with a gunshot wound.

"Good eyes. But I think I'll g-" They praised, but stopped by Señora Salcedo.

"Consider yourself under arrest." She showed them the paper for the S Class Mission. It was a vast reward. I mean, the Deep Forest is where the number one hero was hit by the meteor. No one knows how it happened, as no one else was there, but the story was quickly covered up by the government.

"Weird, isn't it? The number one hero supposedly died here, but no one knows where the body went. A meteor came and is nowhere to be found." Mrs. Staller held a gun right at their head.

"Trust me, I didn't do it. I just started working here a year ago. I don't even know about any heroes that you're talking about." Knowing if someone lies or not, Señora Salcedo moved the gun away from them.

"It checks out. You're around the same age as our rookies. Have you ever met your boss?"

"No. None of us have." They told her.

"Us? There's more of you?" Mandy wrapped bandages around the wound they got, since they would be a good source of information.

"Well, I'm over the part with the memories. That's my power. But, there's 2 others besides me. Since we haven't had proper introductions, my name is..." They began, then pausing.

"What's wrong?"

"…I actually can't remember my name. That's kind of weird."

"I'm pretty sure our rookies can handle you guys. Amazing for their age."

"I can just shoot them." Mrs. Staller stated.

"No!"

"Then we need to find out who's fighting who." James was facing off against one of the members.

"We have someone named Walter, I guess your names are a little similar." He stated, sending a lightning bolt towards him. He dodged it and countered with a lightning bolt of his own.

"Well isn't that spectacular." William responded. So far, every attack James sent was copied perfectly and used against him. Unless one of them ran out of energy, this would basically be a never-ending battle.

"I need notoriety points to boost my chances at becoming a pro, so it would be great if you could join us." James brought up.

"Sure, I don't mind." He agreed, so they went on their way back to the arena. Despite it raining, Kendall was circling the island in full phoenix form, trying to find anyone that needs help fighting. Of course, there's only one fight left. Another villain going against two almost heroes.

"That's some nice powers you have there." The villain said, tapping Alex on the shoulder. Even though she wasn't touched, Amy had the urge to blast them at close range. When the smoke cleared, it revealed them blocking with Alex's steel.

"Okay, now you're really getting on my nerves!" Amy shouted, going on a full-on blast assault. They added more steel the more times they were blasted.

"Are you using the same tactic as Madison?"

"I created that myself! She stole that from me!" After a few more blasts, they eventually moved out of the way. The steel conveniently went off, which caught the flute's attention.

"Time limit." Alex said.

"Yeah, I know. If I were you, I'd join us before we destroy you." Amy told them. They weren't phased by it much.

"Excuse me? It's before you destroy them. I'm not getting my hands dirty because of a fight you started."

"Way to ruin a threat."

"I'll join, sure. But make me the section leader of the altos." They bargained. Amy pointed towards the direction of the arena.

"I'm sure we can negotiate that. Let's just get out of this place."

BRICK OF SOUND

Chapter 30

DUE TO A PROMISE

Madison woke up. Not on Earth, but some other place. It was similar to the void, yet more empty. She woke up in a cold sweat and began looking around to analyze the place.

"What the..." Suddenly, a bright light began glowing from across from her. Using logic, she got up and head straight for it. She stopped. That person from the Room of Mind and Truth reappeared. They held out their hand for Madison.

"As long as we're breathing, we won't let anything happen to you."

Flashback Begin

"What about you, Madison?" Chloe asked her. The group were discussing their number one goal. Madison pointed at herself in pride.

"The same as you guys, to become the number one hero!"

"Everyone has a reason to want to be the best hero. So far, everyone except you." Mandy pointed out, which made the currently flute look down.

"...you're right. I can create a reason on the way. But so far, the only thing that's close to a reason is for me not to die. Basically, I want to become number one, so I can't die until then!"

"So, you're saying it's perfectly fine for you to die after then?" Allie asked. Madison's expression went blank.

"No questions."

Flashback End

Blue steam came out of Madison's mouth, as she began waking up. She barely opened her eyes, since she was still in pain.

"Section Leader! You're alive!" Chloe exclaimed, picking up her hand. Madison woke up a bit more, gripping her hand. Allie was healing her previously but stopped when she saw the steam. Unable to move her body much, Madison simply flashed a grin.

"Yo." After being in shock and surprise, Allie hugged Madison, which woke the tenor up completely.

"You can't just die on us!" She told her, practically squeezing her back to death.

"I will if you don't stop!" Madison managed to get out, so Allie stopped. Kim was crying watching this.

"Alex, quit summoning onions." She told Alex, who was also crying a little.

"I can't create onions, idiot!" He responded.

"Both of you are idiots." Ash said to the both of them. Chloe helped Madison get up.

"How did you come back, daughter?" Ms. Stevens asked the tenor.

"I saw a light, and I tried to go towards it. I think I got lost." Madison explained. Ms. Martinez sighed.

"Well, we can't do the midterms anymore. So, I guess you guys pass. This calls for celebration!" They left the arena on the island, maybe as a gift to them. Since they were famous now, they could just get some other people to build a new one.

Speaking of fame, Madison met a fan while on the way to the Band House Extended.

"You're Madison, right? The tenor?" They asked Madison, who responded with finger guns while still being carried by Chloe.

"The tenor of your dreams, of course! Want my autograph?" They nodded excitedly, handing her a piece of paper. She took out a pen and wrote 'Prez' on the paper.

"Thanks a lot!" They ran off, leaving the group there.

"Being the president of Single Town really pays off. I've given my first autograph away, and I've never been on a class mission." Madison said.

"Aside from the Z Class Mission, you were gone every single time we had chances of doing one." Mandy responded.

"Let me be in my moment." Once they made it back, the party was held in the Band House Extended. Usually when there's a party on the surface, Mary would appear.

"Come on, enjoy the party! You're going to heal eventually, so why not have fun now?" Mary questioned the tenor, who was leaning on a wall.

"Seeing you makes my legs hurt." Her entire lower half was wrapped in bandages, despite not being damaged there. It might be from her blasting herself in the stomach, which could have brought out more pain from the scars on her legs.

"Hey, you paid me, so I provided. That's how it works."

"I didn't pay you; you broke into my house for no reason, then stole my first limited edition Ms. Martinez figure! Chasing you is not the easiest thing in the world!"

"It's not stealing if I gave it back."

"Alright, it's time for a meeting! We have to discuss what we do before we go back to school." Ms. Martinez called out to everyone in the room. They gathered around a table with 3 options on it.

"We either take a break, go on a bunch of missions, or do one big mission." Allie explained. Madison raised her hand.

"The big mission! We have a lot of people on our side now, so it'll be a piece of cake!"

"I agree with the nerd. She has Single Town, which has an entire army, and we could blow whatever quest out of the water." Mandy said. Ms. Martinez crossed her arms.

"It's the Z Class Mission that no one has ever beaten. In a separate dimension no one has access to. Are you guys sure of this?" Being the prideful demon princess that she is, Allie simply shrugged.

"I mean, we beat one easily. If we do this one, we'll definitely get a reward." Ms. Martinez turned to the number three hero.

"If the kids want to do it, then so be it. I'm sure it'll be a fun trip, too!" Ms. Stevens responded.

"Then that settles it. Our last trip before we prepare hard for H.G.P.E will be to the mythical Bronzeland!"

AVAILABLE NOW!
DON'T MISS OUT ON THESE RELEASES BY
MADISON PATE
BRICK OF SOUND
BY
MADISON PATE
BRICK OF SOUND 2
MADISON PATE
AVAILABLE WHEREVER BOOKS ARE SOLD
WWW.TANDJPUBLISHERS.COM